The Disappearance of Swenson's Secretary

A HAROLD OBER MYSTERY

The Disappearance of Swenson's Secretary

A HAROLD OBER MYSTERY

by J. D. West

A Golden Age Detective Novel

Post Office Box 600725, Newton, MA 02460

10   9   8   7   6   5   4   3   2   1

For

Phyllis Westberg

and

Craig Tenney

The Disappearance of Swenson's Secretary

1

"NOW HOW DOES it sound?"

Max rolled the page up in his typewriter. "'I never noticed the stars before. I always thought of them as great big diamonds that belonged to someone. Now they frighten me. They make me feel that it was all a dream, all my youth.' 'It was a dream,' said John quietly."

Fitzgerald wrinkled his aquiline nose. His sparkling green eyes shone with concentration. "'It *was* a dream.' That still doesn't quite bring it off."

The low lamps cast shadows on the muted brown wallpaper of the spacious corner office. A symphony of intermittent honking and voices twelve floors below on Madison Avenue rose through the window nearest Harold Ober's desk, perpetually open a crack to admit fresh air. The windowpane reflected Ober's expressionless face and benevolent brow as he spoke slowly into the phone, his low, deliberate voice calmly declining a lunch invitation from an editor at Harper & Brothers for Friday, which was his reading day, a sacred time dedicated solely to reading his clients' manuscripts at his home in Connecticut. He pursed his lips as he hung up and smoothed the crest of hair most men in their fifties didn't possess.

Fitzgerald took another run at it. "'It *was* a dream,' said John quietly. 'Everybody's youth is a dream, a form of chemical madness.'"

Max's fingers flew across the typewriter keys.

"That's nice," Ober said. "Brings it across."

Fitzgerald appeared from behind the trifold screen made from reclaimed wine barrel wood, sold by an enterprising Hudson River valley vintner at the start of Volstead, that separated Max's corner perch from the rest of the office. The divider had been given as a gift from a former client who had drunkenly obliterated the previous screen, but also as a comment on Ober's fastidiousness, which included abstention from drink. Fitzgerald plopped down in one of the two chairs positioned across from Ober's enormous walnut desk. He stretched his languid frame as if after a day's work. "I told Mencken he could have a first look for the *Smart Set*."

"Fine, Scott," Ober agreed. "Max, please have Wilson deliver a copy after lunch."

"Yes, sir."

Fitzgerald yawned expansively. "Zelda and I want you and Anne to come out to Great Neck."

"It would be our pleasure. Anne keeps the schedule, as you know. I'll mention it to her."

Fitzgerald had hardly excused himself for lunch with his editor at Scribner when the film agent Peter Swenson knocked twice on the doorjamb. Swenson was in New York from Los Angeles on his annual trip east to make the rounds with publishers and agents to discuss any interesting manuscripts that might translate well to film. He glided into the room like a sailboat, his close-cropped white hair and bronzed face glowing in the low lighting.

"Great to see you, Swanie." Ober stood up behind his desk and they shook hands vigorously.

"I passed Fitzgerald in the lobby," Swenson said. "His latest sounds like a real humdinger."

"He's trying to break out of the mold of his making. His words."

"What chameleons writers are, right? I guess you and I depend on that fact." Swenson peered at his watch.

"How was your voyage?"

"Long," he answered.

Swenson eyed his watch again.

"Are you running a little behind?" Ober asked.

"No, not at all. It's just . . . I brought my secretary along—she has a friend in New York—and when she didn't show up for breakfast at my hotel, I left word for her to meet me here."

A warm breeze carrying the first hints of autumn filtered through the open window.

"Is she staying with her friend?" Ober asked.

"No, at a women's hotel over on Lexington. I rang her room this morning, but no answer."

"The Byrne Hotel?"

"That's the one."

"Is she reliable?"

"Like a clock," Swenson said worriedly. "It's very unlike her."

"What about the friend?"

"My secretary lived briefly in New York before moving to the coast, and I assumed it was a reunion of sorts. I didn't catch any name."

"If you'd like, we can stroll over to her hotel and ask the concierge."

"Oh, no. Perhaps she's on her way. We can start without her."

The phone on Max's desk buzzed and he answered it with his customary flourish, not unlike a stage magician juggling a set of lit torches.

"Miss Jeannette Barnes is here to see you," the receptionist informed him.

A very worried Miss Barnes catapulted from the red leather chair in reception when she saw Max. She extended a tiny gloved hand as Max smiled into her pinched face. The new receptionist, a Jamaican woman in her sixties sent over from the temp agency, continued to leaf through the copy of *Life* magazine at her desk. Ober employed temporary receptionists to prevent gossip about his business from being spread, and every week a new face showed itself at the reception desk.

"I'm a Domino," Miss Barnes said. "Lily Cotton said you might be able to help me."

The Dominoes were an acting troupe that staged plays forbidden by the Comstock Law after hours in the Domino sugar warehouse in Williamsburg, Brooklyn. Domino plays were risqué, and the crowds were mostly the wealthy elite dressed down, under cover as the working class. Lily Cotton, whose day job was as a bookseller at Scribner Book Store, was one of the star players.

At the mention of the Dominoes, Max ushered Miss Barnes out of the receptionist's earshot and down the short hall, lined with Ober clients' books, to the spartan office belonging to Ober's partner, Miss Doling.

A hopper window high above Miss Doling's desk was the only source of natural light. Max reached for the lamp in the corner, which threw a flare of light across the neat shelves filled with books and rubber-banded manuscripts. Mr. Ober was singular in the publishing world for his elevation of his former secretary to full-fledged agent with her own client list, but he impressed upon Max how important it was to shield Miss Doling from their extracurricular activities. Max was grateful that Miss Barnes's unexpected appearance had coincided with Miss Doling's reading day. He prompted Miss Barnes, and she gushed a worried tale about her boyfriend, who had seemingly gone missing. The boyfriend, a Philip Slater, lived and worked in the city during the week but spent the weekends at his mother's house upstate. It had been more than a week since he'd called on Miss Barnes, the first time that had happened.

"When did you last see him?"

"Over a week ago. We were supposed to go to a party together, but I got sick and he went alone. That was a week ago Friday."

"Where does he stay in the city?"

"At the Williams Club. He was living down on Wall Street, where he works, but he had a dispute with his roommate, so he's been staying at his club."

"What was the nature of the dispute?"

Miss Barnes shrugged her thin shoulders. "He never told me."

"What does he do for a living on Wall Street?"

She shrugged again, adding a wince. "Something to do with bonds."

Max narrowed his gaze, then let the vague answer pass.

"Can you provide the names of some of his associates or friends?"

She said that she didn't know any. "He sometimes mentioned someone named Andrew," she said, "but it was never clear to me who that was."

Max raised an eyebrow and then let it float back into place.

"Where do you reside?"

"I board on the Lower East Side," she answered, pleased to be able to give a concrete answer.

Max asked a series of questions meant to elicit a physical profile, and Miss Barnes answered them eagerly, as if each was the key to solving the mystery as to where the boyfriend had gone.

"I brought this photograph." Miss Barnes handed him a black-and-white photo. It was a picture of a tall, fair-haired figure with a disapproving face standing on a beach. The subject was shading his eyes, and the entire photo was slightly out of focus. "It's not very good, I'm afraid. Philip is the camera enthusiast, but one can't take one's own picture."

Max smiled, a kindness Miss Barnes clearly appreciated.

"What's the address of that party he wanted to take you to?"

She didn't know, only that it was on the Upper East Side. Max sent her away with a promise to see what he could do. His employer had an aversion to domestic cases like these, rightly concluding that they resolved themselves one way or another given time, and Max recognized that his interest in the case was being driven more by Lily Cotton's having recommended him than any hope of finding the disappeared boyfriend. He knew too well how men could treat women, and the outline of the matter at hand did nothing to dissuade his pessimism. Still, it was worth a visit to his old friend in Brooklyn at the very least.

After spending the rest of the day carefully transferring the royalty rates and other pertinent information from the month's new contracts onto the color-coded cards Ober used to see a snapshot of each contract rather than having to dig out the actual contract when necessary, Max plummeted into the fetid subway station at Union Square in the gloaming and emerged at North Seventh and Bedford in Williamsburg in darkness. Cool air swept off the East River as he made his way down Bedford and took South First toward Kent Avenue, the breeze tinged with the sickly smell of the sugar factory. Downriver, the hulking Brooklyn Bridge was shrouded in cloud cover, its ghostly expanse running back to the civilized shores of Manhattan.

Max remembered from his short stint as a Domino—Lily had convinced him to take a part in their production of *Lysistrata*, put on in a show of solidarity with the Moscow Art Theatre, which had been raided and shuttered after performing the play—that Monday night was rehearsal night, but also that after the grueling Saturday and Sunday performances the cast generally gathered in the cafeteria at the back of the warehouse, mostly to smoke cigarettes and pass flasks of whatever bootleg whiskey was available. Smoking was forbidden, but the night watchman could be bribed with a pull of whiskey, and the Dominoes were careful about pocketing their butts and spent matches. A haze rose from the wooden picnic tables, and Max was glad to see so many friendly and familiar faces. A round of huzzahs went up, echoing in the cavernous space, which Max acknowledged. Only Lily, tall and willowy, swinging her legs from the loading dock against the far wall that served as the makeshift stage, remained silent. She smiled and exhaled a plume of smoke in Max's direction.

"Whato, stranger," she said. She flipped the braid of her long, dark hair over her shoulder. "You don't waste any time."

"That's how we do it in the big city."

"Mr. Big City," she said, drawing on her cigarette. "That's you."

He sat next to Lily on the cold concrete loading dock, the sweet, spiced smell of oranges and licorice he associated with her filling his mouth. Lily was the only person he'd confided his secret to: that his father had given him a year to pursue his ambition to be a writer, a talent he quickly realized he didn't possess when he took the job at Harold Ober Associates. But he loved New York City and its promise of endless reinvention, and knew he would never return to Cincinnati. His father's deadline had lapsed some time ago, and he hadn't spoken to either of his parents in years because of it.

"I take it Jeannette is still trying to find her no-account boyfriend."

"She didn't quite describe him in those terms."

"She wouldn't. She's too smitten," Lily said.

"Spend any time with the boyfriend? Can you tell me anything more than his name and rank?"

"Not really. He liked to be alone with Jeannette. That type. Not good in a crowd, which God knows Jeannette isn't either. He was always taking her to the movies, sometimes Coney Island. They took a hansom cab ride around Central Park once, and you'd think listening to her that they'd taken a rocket ship to the moon."

An explosion of laughter went up at one of the picnic tables, and a loud actor with a silly face Max didn't recognize jumped on top of the table and mimicked a sultry dance, to the delight of everyone.

"Where is Jeannette from?" Max asked.

Lily shrugged. "Somewhere not here."

"Remember that thing you told me once? About someone inviting actresses to posh parties uptown?"

Lily trained her deep-blue eyes on him. "You an impresario now?"

He laughed and shook his head.

"It happens sometimes," she said. "You know, men with money like what they see and don't want to be just a face in the crowd."

"You ever go to any?"

She regarded him, teasing out the moment. "Maybe."

"Is it all *Girl in the Red Velvet Swing* stuff?"

She punched him in the arm harder than he deserved. He took it.

"Those were the rumors, anyway."

"I'm not saying," she said. Another smirk, but this one only half strength.

"I'm more interested in those handing out invitations. Any of them residents of the Upper East Side?"

She lit a fresh cigarette with the embers of her last. "One comes to mind. A real smoothy. The son of someone who is someone."

"Know a name?"

She jumped down, brushing ash from her white linen blouse.

"I do, but you didn't hear it from me."

<u>2</u>

OBER AND MAX APPROACHED SWENSON, who was pacing the lobby of the Byrne Hotel, his heels clacking against the green and black tiles. The lobby was inexplicably overgrown with ferns.

"Thank you for coming," he said. "I didn't know who else to call."

"Still no word?" Ober asked. He removed his hat.

The hotel manager, a compact man with smooth white skin and a brisk manner, appeared. "I checked with the staff, and her key has been out overnight." The manager delivered the news with gusto, as if it were good news, but Swenson's unchanged look of worry refuted the manager's supposition.

"May we see her room?" Ober asked.

"That would be highly irregular," the manager said officiously. He gripped both lapels of his suit jacket—spun in the same green color as the tile floor—and rocked on his heels in an attempt to quell further discussion on the matter.

"Would you prefer us to report Miss Salzman missing and have the police open her room?" Swenson asked pointedly.

The hotel manager twitched, considering.

"This way, gentlemen."

The dark-green river of carpet muffled their footsteps as they approached the room. A chambermaid with raven-black hair and a listing stride smiled as she passed them, her arms loaded with fresh white towels.

The manager gave a short rap on the door. No answer. He knocked again, and then unlocked the door and replaced the master key in his pocket all in one short motion. The jangle of his keys was the only audible sound as Swenson pushed his way into the immaculate room, followed by Ober's deliberate step, Max trailing. The manager remained in the doorway by force of professional habit.

The room was small but not cramped, and decorated without ornamentation: A firm bed and mattress took up most of the room, the yellow quilted bedspread the same color as the upholstered headboard. A square wooden nightstand supported a black metal reading lamp. Above the lamp, a print of a dressage horse caught Max's eye. Swenson pulled open the closet door and found it empty save for two wooden hangers.

"Are you sure this is the right room?" he asked.

"Yes, sir," the manager answered.

"But it's clear no one is occupying it."

The manager shrugged.

A weak light pulsed through the heavy curtains, and Ober threw them open to a view of the fire escape and not much else. The well-lit room looked for all the world like a postcard of a New York City hotel room.

"Did she make any phone calls?" Ober asked the manager.

The manager seemed relieved to have reason to excuse himself from the increasingly uncomfortable scene. "I'll try to find out."

"He won't be gone long," Ober said. He instructed Swenson to check all the drawers and for Max to conduct a careful sweep under the bed and pillows. Ober switched the light on in the bathroom, the pungent smell of bleach burning his nose. The lack of any trace of Miss Salzman was puzzling. As he flicked the switch off, a glint of white light was cast against the pink tile under the bathroom window. Ober captured the light with an open hand and then traced it back to its source, a metal compact case wedged between the base of the porcelain sink and the wall. As he bent to retrieve it, his fingers ran across the initials AK engraved in Cyrillic on the cover.

"What do you make of this?" he asked Swenson.

Swenson turned the compact over in his hands. "Might've been left by a previous guest. Those aren't her initials. The drawers are empty too. What a mystery."

Swenson passed the compact back to Ober, who handed it to Max. "Put this in your pocket."

"It's almost as if she's vanished," Swenson said.

"Do you think it's possible she went to stay with her friend?" Ober asked.

"Anything is possible, I suppose. But why wouldn't she let me know?"

"Maybe the friend involved her in some kind of emergency."

"She surely would've left word," Swenson said. "Miss Salzman is one of the most efficient secretaries at the firm."

"Do you know if she was friendly with any other secretaries? Perhaps someone knows more about her plans while she was in New York."

A pained look crept across Swenson's face. "That's not something I would know, unfortunately."

The manager materialized in the doorway again with a clever-looking girl of medium height, flaxen hair cut at a severe angle, at his side. "Excuse me, gentlemen. I'm informed by Miss Kennedy here that no calls were made from or received in this room"—Miss Kennedy's green eyes widened at the mention of her testimony—"but that her brother called on her an hour or so after she checked in on Sunday."

"At least we know she checked in," Max said.

"But she doesn't have a brother," Swenson remarked.

"Would she have mentioned it if she did?" Ober asked.

"Probably not," Swenson said, "but it happened to come up that she doesn't have any family at all. She grew up in an orphanage somewhere in Russia. She came to America the first chance she got."

Ober turned to Miss Kennedy. "Can you describe the man claiming to be her brother?"

"We were extremely busy yesterday," Miss Kennedy explained. "Normally, there would be two of us helping guests check in, but

Miss Goodman had another one of her spells and at the last minute called in to say she would be out."

"Does this happen often?" Ober asked.

"Miss Goodman was one of our best," the manager said, "but over the last year she has become a touch unreliable."

"She was excellent at the holidays," Miss Kennedy interjected.

The manager gave a benevolent look. "Occasionally she returns to her previous form, yes."

"You were giving us a description of the brother," Swenson reminded her impatiently.

"Well and yes," Miss Kennedy said. "He was a very nice gentleman in a gabardine suit, with a canary-yellow shirt and a pink satin pocket square. No hat. I thought it was unusual he wasn't wearing a hat when the rest of his suit was so carefully constructed."

Max touched the compact in his pocket and watched his employer quiz Miss Kennedy.

"What about his physical description?"

"He was tall. Darkish face, cloudy, you know."

"Cloudy?"

"He didn't look like he smiled much. Sort of washed out looking, too. He had enormous hands. And he'd just had a manicure."

"What did he say to you?"

"He said he wanted to surprise his sister and asked if he could have her room number. I told him that we don't allow men in the rooms."

"Did you think it was unusual that he knew his sister was in town, but that he didn't know her room number?"

Miss Kennedy twisted shyly on the carpet. "I couldn't say, sir. But he was annoyed at not being able to go to her room."

"Annoyed how?"

"He sort of hissed with his teeth. Chewed his tongue like they sometimes do when they want to say something nasty to you."

"Could this have been the friend she was meeting?" Ober asked Swenson.

Swenson shook his head. "I definitely had the impression it was a woman."

"Is it possible she was perhaps not telling the truth, to shield you?"

Swenson sighed. "At this juncture, anything is possible, I suppose."

"He *didn't* just have a manicure," Miss Kennedy said suddenly. "I'm confusing that detail with another gentleman who called the previous morning. The brother actually had dirty fingernails." She paused. "And I might be confusing the suit, too."

A wave of tension went around the room. Ober smiled delicately.

"It sounds like you were very busy," he offered.

"When you're checking guests in, you're sure to look them in the eyes and smile and welcome them, but when men are in the lobby, they're mostly asking for directions or mistaking the front entrance for the delivery entrance around back, so you don't take too much notice. But I'm right about the brother not wearing a hat. And now the dirty fingernails." She clamped her hands to her face. "Although now I'm thinking that was the emergency plumber we called two nights ago. He wasn't wearing a hat because he wasn't wearing a suit. That makes sense, right?" She looked desperately from face to face.

"Don't trouble yourself," Ober said calmly. "It's almost certain that Miss Salzman does not have a brother. I think we can assume that, anyway."

"I'm sorry not to be more useful, sir," Miss Kennedy said, both to Ober and to the manager, who put his hand on her back and walked her down the hall.

"There's nothing here," Swenson sighed. "I don't know whether to be worried or annoyed."

"Something is definitely wrong," Ober mused.

"But her luggage is gone. Wherever she went, she went willingly."

"Could be," Ober said in a way Max recognized that meant *Maybe yes and maybe no.* He knew Ober thought to the contrary when Ober asked him to find Wilson and have him watch the lobby.

3

MAX CROSSED FIFTH AVENUE to the limestone and red brick mansion on the corner of Eighty-Second Street. He was not looking forward to the questions he needed to put to its resident, Franklin Dixon, the sixth-wealthiest man in New York. The Dixon fortune had been built on shipping and railroad enterprises generations before. Franklin Dixon's proximity to the Metropolitan Museum of Art was no accident: He was one of the city's biggest philanthropists and as close to the mayor as one could be without being related.

The first-floor maid caught sight of Max before he could work up the courage to knock. A pretty, amiable face appeared in the iron and glass door. The door shuddered when she swung it open.

"Yes?"

Max waffled about asking for Mr. Dixon or his son, Leslie, directly. Both were going to deny knowledge of any illicit dealings, but Ober had taught him how instructive face-to-face encounters could be for the purposes of deduction.

"Is Mr. Leslie Dixon at home?"

"Are you expected?"

Max hesitated, and the maid instinctively pushed the door in front of her like a shield, her amiability vanishing.

"I'm calling on behalf of a friend of a friend."

"Name?"

"Max Harding."

"One moment please."

The maid closed the door. She reappeared minutes later to inform him that no one was home.

Max put on his lost-child face.

"Are you live-in?"

The maid screwed up her face. "I am."

"Were you here two weekends ago?"

A cloud passed across her smooth features. "I've told the police everything I know, I'm sorry." She averted her eyes and closed the door. As her dainty figure receded behind the glass, she paused, turned toward him, and grimaced, before disappearing down a hallway.

The stoicism of the adjoining brownstones—an entire block's worth of wealth and silence—told Max he'd get the same reception if he knocked on all the doors along Fifth Avenue, so he entered Central Park at the carousel and walked down through the barren landscape to the Pond. The first fall offerings from the canopy of trees overhead skimmed the water. He crossed Fifty-Ninth Street to the Plaza Hotel, zeroing in on the big, friendly doorman clad in royal blue who was shepherding a plump woman and her child up the red-carpeted stairs toward the glittering entranceway. Oliver Parker, a former Domino, waved when he saw Max. His bulky body seemed ill suited for the uniform swaddling his frame.

"Hey ho," he said cheerfully.

They exchanged pleasantries and remarked again about the proximity of their jobs, and how they should have lunch sometime, the way acquaintances who aren't really friends often do.

"I went back and saw the Dominoes," Max said.

"How is Lily? She recommended a great book, which I promptly never read."

"As always. I'm working on something for a friend of hers. Know anything about the police being called to Eighty-Second Street a couple of weekends ago?"

"The guy who went off the roof?"

Max didn't know what he'd expected, but it wasn't that.

"At Franklin Dixon's place?"

Oliver glanced over his shoulder. "Hey, no names."

Max remembered that Dixon had been a regular at the Men's Bar at the Plaza before it was shuttered by the Volstead Act.

"Who went over?"

"Cops aren't saying."

"The cops know?"

"They asked me about it a couple of days after. First I'd heard of it. Wasn't in the papers."

"These people are in the papers only when they want to be. So, no description even?"

"Nada." He tipped his cap at a squat man in a gabardine suit who rushed out of the hotel entrance, bounding down the stairs toward Fifth Avenue. "Cops said he was arguing with someone earlier at the party. That's who they're looking for. You should see the parade of pretty girls that stream into that place, boy." He grinned salaciously. "They take pictures, I heard."

"Pictures?"

"You know. The kinds of pictures druggists develop in their back rooms." Oliver nodded knowingly, but it was the first Max had heard of it.

"You get a card from the cops?"

Oliver reached into his jacket for his wallet and produced Sergeant Roosevelt's card. Max smiled. Sergeant Roosevelt had been the sole beneficiary of any illegal activity Ober uncovered. Roosevelt's involvement in this case, whatever it was, felt like a sign of some kind, even though Max felt no closer to the truth about what had happened to Jeannette Barnes's boyfriend.

4

STANDING UNDER THE VAULTED CEILING in Scribner Book
Store, light streaming down from the clerestory windows, one was
immediately put in mind of a cathedral, the conversation in hushed
tones from the congregants gathered around the tables of books
lending authenticity to the impression.

Max caught sight of Lily, her hair swept up fashionably, as she
climbed a wooden ladder in the fiction section. She was wearing
what she called her bookseller's uniform: black sweater, plaid skirt,
black tights, and shoes sensible enough for climbing. Her ability to
dramatically transform her appearance always astounded him.

Max came up behind her. "Excuse me, I'm looking for a book
recommendation."

Lily flashed a sarcastic smile as she backed down the ladder.
"Lemme guess. You're too embarrassed to ask for the new Zane Grey."

"I haven't finished the last one, actually."

She trained her vividly blue eyes on him. "Aren't they all generally
the same?"

"I thought booksellers were supposed to suppress their personal
opinions about the books they sell."

"You'd be surprised about some of the opinions around here.
And not just about books."

She flashed another smile, a relief. Her deadpan delivery made it
hard to tell if she was ever kidding or not. "You here with the boss?"

Max shook his head. The publishing offices of Scribner occupied the top floors of the building, and on occasion Max would loiter in the bookstore while Ober attended to business upstairs.

"I have a galley of a new book I think you might like," Lily said. "As a sensitive young man, I mean."

Before Max could think of a rejoinder, she was gone, and she reappeared with the item in question, the hotly anticipated first novel from Fitzgerald's literary discovery, Ernest Hemingway. Max had previously shared with Lily the drama surrounding the book: Hemingway had written the novella *The Torrents of Spring* in a couple of weeks in order to induce his old publisher to reject it, freeing him to publish his novel *The Sun Also Rises* with Scribner.

"I hope it won't scandalize you," Lily said.

"It can't be more scandalous than what I need to ask you," Max said. He could feel a heat working its way to his brow.

Lily crossed her arms and smiled. "Intrigued."

"What was the name of that bookseller with the goatee—"

"Luke."

"Right, Luke. You remember you told me he was into some weird stuff?"

"I deny being a gossip."

"Oh, this wasn't gossip," Max assured her. "It was just . . . informational."

"Thank you for rescuing my honor."

Max gave a short bow. "Anyway, you once mentioned that Luke needed some pictures developed, the kind you couldn't readily take to a photo lab."

Lily considered him. "Are you an amateur photographer now?"

Max blushed. "I'm not asking for me."

Lily's blue eyes widened. "Not for the boss, I hope," she whispered. The very idea of Max's Protestant boss with such a hobby sent them both into a fit of giggles. Her eyes widened even more. "Not Jeannette's thing?" Her sultry mouth opened in disbelief.

"Not sure yet," Max said. "Just looking for some leads. I heard druggists sometimes develop the kinds of photos we're talking about. Is that what your coworker did?"

"He never named a druggist in particular. Just hinted that that's how he was developing his art pictures. That's what he called them."

"Any idea where the druggist was located?"

"He didn't work here that long. Remember Mrs. Lubbe caught him stealing?"

"Money?"

"Books. Ones with weird titles."

At the mention of Mrs. Lubbe's name, her lithe but capable-looking frame appeared in the aisle. Max tucked the Hemingway galley into his messenger bag.

"Thank you for the recommendation," Max said loudly as Mrs. Lubbe passed, casting a watchful eye in Lily's direction.

"You'll love it," Lily said as loudly, waiting for Mrs. Lubbe to clear the aisle.

"Ring me if you think of something else," Max said.

"There is one thing," Lily said, lowering her voice. "Someone who might know something."

"Another prurient-minded bookseller?"

"Actually, someone closer to you than to me."

"How close?"

"You know that writer Ober represents who wears that black cape?"

Max knew whom she meant, James Fayette, though he was a client of Miss Doling's, not Ober's. Fayette was attempting a novel based on the life of Mary Rogers, the beautiful cigar store girl whose murder inspired Edgar Allan Poe's short story. Max, and everyone else, considered him an oddball, but within the realm of writerly oddity. This new wrinkle surprised him.

"I know him, yes."

"I overheard him talking to a friend in the photography section one day about how he has a druggist on the Lower East Side who handles all of his prints."

Max looked doubtful.

"That could mean anything. You're too influenced by the cape."

Lily shrugged. "Suit yourself. You're the one who asked."

"I just mean it's not really proof of anything."

"Of course. Got any other questions you don't want to hear the answers to?" Lily asked sarcastically. "You never come in here for my true expertise."

"Oh, that reminds me." Max produced the compact from the missing secretary's bathroom. "Anything unusual about this?" he asked.

Lily ran her fingers over the engraved initials, then popped the cover, revealing the well-worn pad of face powder. She clicked the compact shut and handed it back. "Just the Cyrillic engraving. Whose initials are they?"

"Not sure. I just found it," Max said casually. "Hoping to return it to the owner."

"Between locating the druggist and locating the owner of her lost cosmetics, I'm amazed you have any time for your paying job."

Max smiled, and was still smiling as Lily was called away to the counter to ring up the purchases of a woman with a high-pitched voice and meticulously arranged hair.

5

MAX PLACED AN ASHTRAY in front of the poet Langston Hughes, who nodded as Max retreated behind his screen. Hughes inhaled deeply and then let the smoke drift from his always-smiling mouth.

"How is the collection coming?" Ober asked.

Hughes rubbed his high forehead, as if trying to will the correct answer.

"When you first suggested a book, I thought I didn't have enough published work, but I see now I've got enough to leave some out."

"More than any poet can ask for."

"Were you straight when you said Mr. Knopf would give me more time on the deadline? I've got some new poems brewing that I might like to include."

"I'm sure it can be arranged."

Hughes tamped his cigarette against the ashtray.

"Max's message was curious. Very mysterious."

"It wasn't meant to be."

"When your agent has his assistant leave a message that he wants to see you, it's usually not good news. I asked a few friends."

Ober smiled. "Such suspicious friends. No, I have an idea for a collaboration, and I thought it best to sit and discuss it."

"You want to write a book together?"

"Not exactly. I have an idea for a book and I'd like you to write it."

"What's the idea?"

"Do you know of Sergeant Roosevelt of the New York Police Department?"

"Of course. The first Negro police officer on the force." Hughes tapped his cigarette against the brass ashtray. "A burden I wouldn't wish on anyone."

"Exactly. You can see how Sergeant Roosevelt's story might make an intriguing book."

Hughes squinted, inhaling again.

"But I'm not a biographer."

"I'm not suggesting a biography, exactly. The story feels much bigger than that to me."

"Perhaps a more well-known writer should take it on. It'll likely be attacked, and unpleasant for a certain segment of the population. I've no reputation to lend it weight."

"Your reputation is growing, believe me."

Hughes deflected the compliment by turning his head and blowing a torrent of smoke toward the opening in the window near Ober's desk.

"I'd love to meet him, in any case."

"That's all I can ask."

The bright visage of Miss Doling appeared in the hallway outside Ober's door and waved at Max, who excused himself. Miss Doling's quiet, languid presence in the office was a source of calm. She was an agreeable woman of middle age whom Max found himself doting over as he used to his mother, though more often than not it was she who was mothering him.

"The receptionist stepped out for a cigarette, and a very upset Miss Barnes called for you," Miss Doling said. "I offered to take a message, but she hung up."

"She's, uh, a new client," Max offered.

"What's the plot?" Miss Doling asked, employing the shorthand they'd developed to talk about the investigative work being conducted out of the office. Max and Miss Doling maintained the fiction that Miss Doling was not in the know, out of loyalty to their boss's wishes.

"Missing boyfriend."

"That's a little ordinary."

"Yes, I said so."

"It doesn't sound like something Mr. Ober would be interested in."

Max flinched, pawing his foot at the carpet. "You're right."

"You're not taking on manuscripts on your own, are you?"

"It's more of a short story," Max answered unconvincingly.

Miss Doling shot him a concerned look.

6

WILSON PULLED ON THE BRIM of his worn plaid ivy cap. The boss had told him to stake out the lobby, and so that's what he'd do. No job was too small for the man who'd hired him away from his previous employer, who'd taken all the money and given Wilson but a taste of it. But Wilson had never seen a quieter hotel. At first the prospect of spending the afternoon in a women's hotel had been tantalizing, but after an hour hiding behind a newspaper, the allure was gone. The manager pretended not to see him, and the glances from the two women working the registration desk were more fearful than anything else. The urge to visit the restroom came and went. He didn't dare leave his post. That was always the moment he was meant to capture, he knew, a lesson from the only time he'd disappointed the boss, that case involving the prep-school kid who had run away from his school. The boss had said it wasn't his fault, it *was* his first stakeout, but Wilson never wanted to feel that useless again.

He hadn't previously considered how boring an afternoon in a hotel lobby could be, the occasional telephoned request from a guest causing a ripple in the otherwise tedious calm. The only real excitement was a boisterous man in a loud suit with an even louder Boston accent who asked for directions to Central Park. One of the women behind the counter made a remark Wilson couldn't hear after the man had left, which caused the other woman to snort in laughter.

The vigil seemed a bust as the five o'clock foot traffic began up and down Lexington Avenue, when a slight woman with a worried face leaked through the entrance.

"Could you please ring Miss Vera Salzman's room?" the woman asked the lone receptionist, who had appeared at shift change. She had an accent Wilson couldn't place. Something guttural, like his uncle after his afternoon drink.

The receptionist checked the register and blinked her wide brown eyes at the woman. She pressed the receiver to her ear. "Who should I say is calling?

"Mrs. Anderson."

The receptionist nodded again. The lobby elevator opened, but no one was inside.

"I'm sorry, there's no answer."

A fearful look crossed Mrs. Anderson's face, and she turned abruptly and trotted out the entrance. Wilson nodded to the receptionist and followed.

The sidewalks teemed with the moving masses scurrying home. Wilson held on to his cap as a gust of wind blew down Lexington Avenue. He trailed Mrs. Anderson, hopping on the same crosstown double-decker bus, though he stood gripping the railing on the rear staircase, intermittently staring at the back of Mrs. Anderson's head and a placard that read: YOUR BUS RIDE WAS PAID FOR YOU COMPLIMENTS OF MAYOR JIMMY WALKER. The newly elected mayor had made reducing the fare from ten cents to a nickel one of his campaign promises. As a result, the buses were often overcrowded, no matter the time of day.

Mrs. Anderson shifted in her seat as the bus approached Seventh Avenue, and Wilson spun off the stairs and made the same transfer onto a downtown bus as his mark did. The ride down Seventh Avenue was interminable, the hulking machine lurching to a stop every few feet. Mrs. Anderson had lucked into a seat at the back of the bus, but Wilson glimpsed her worried face in the driver's rearview mirror now and again. The giant billboards for Arrow collars, Camel cigarettes, and Chevrolet in Times Square didn't register as she stared straight ahead, lost in thought. As the bus turned left onto Fourteenth Street and continued south on Broadway, Wilson wondered if the next leg of their journey would involve swimming to Staten Island. He was resigned to the fact that it would take him twice as long to get home to Spuyten Duyvil tonight.

The towering spire of the Woolworth Building loomed, guiding the bus to a halting stop beneath it. Mrs. Anderson trundled up the aisle, and Wilson waited a beat before following, easily mixing in with the crowd of homebound municipal workers who slaved away at nearby City Hall and the various court buildings.

Mrs. Anderson crossed herself as she approached Saint Paul's and made her way up Vesey Street, an avenue lined with lodging houses. Wilson passed an orgiastic display of fruit and nuts and fish, glancing away from the dead rabbits swinging in a storefront above a tray of pigeons whose wide eyes gleamed in the fading sunlight. Mrs. Anderson passed under a window with a sign announcing TRUTH SEEKER, ONE FLIGHT UP just as a steam whistle bellowed from somewhere on the Hudson River. She reached into her purse and disappeared through the door of a subterranean apartment. Her sudden absence after hours of surveillance spooked Wilson, and he panicked that he'd lost her. But a handwritten slip of paper tacked under the doorbell spelled out her last name, and Wilson noted the address.

"Can I help you?" The voice startled Wilson and he flinched. A tall, gawky man smartly dressed peered down at him.

"N-no, I—" Wilson stammered.

"Remove yourself from my doorstep, then," the man said, waiting impatiently until Wilson moved down the street and began the long reverse journey home.

7

HAROLD OBER PERCHED PRECARIOUSLY on the edge of the tiny wicker chair. Mrs. Anderson sat across from him on a quilt-covered divan, propped up by a stack of dusty multicolored pillows, which allowed her dainty feet to touch the floor. Behind her, through a gauzy white curtain, the foot traffic along Vesey could be seen from the knees down. The garden apartment was cluttered with shelves of knickknacks and framed photos, and Mrs. Anderson's indecisive face glanced nervously from item to item.

"Are you sure it's not my husband you wish to speak to?" she asked hopefully. "He's left for work."

Ober had waited until he was sure the husband was safely at work before he paid his visit to Vesey Street.

"What does your husband do for a living, if you don't mind my asking?"

"He's a civil engineer. He's working for Wilgus."

Ober detected a note of pride in her voice. Wilgus's transformation not only of the great rail station at Forty-Second Street, but also of the train yard that stretched north to midtown into a wide avenue of luxury homes along Park Avenue, was followed closely in the papers. "My office is near all that work," Ober said conversationally, but Mrs. Anderson only nodded. "It is actually you I wanted to speak to. About a friend of yours, Miss Vera Salzman. From California?"

Mrs. Anderson gave a startled look and then glanced away again. Ober noticed that she was in all likelihood a number of years younger than she presented herself.

"I don't know anyone in California."

Mrs. Anderson folded her hands in her lap and remained stock-still.

Ober smiled and gingerly uncrossed and recrossed his legs, the wicker chair shimmying under his weight.

"You weren't at the Byrne Hotel yesterday calling on Miss Salzman?"

"I was home all day."

"You weren't supposed to have dinner with Miss Salzman?"

"I told you, I don't know who that is, so I could hardly have dinner plans with her."

A truck barreled down Vesey Street, rattling the window.

"A funny view," Ober said.

"You get used to it," Mrs. Anderson said.

Ober surveyed the room, taking in the bric-a-brac, all mementos of New York City: a miniature model of the Statue of Liberty, a souvenir plate in a stand touting New York as a "City of Wonders," a snow globe depicting ice-skaters in Central Park.

"How long have you lived here?"

"A few years."

"And before that?"

"I don't mean to be rude, but what business is that of yours?"

Ober smiled. "I thought you might want to talk about something other than your being at the Byrne Hotel yesterday asking after Miss Salzman. It isn't a coincidence that I'm here this morning, Mrs. Anderson. And it isn't only on my behalf, but also her employer's, who wishes to know the whereabouts of his secretary."

Mrs. Anderson stared at him straight in the eye. "Before here I lived in a town outside Moscow."

"How did you and your husband meet?"

"His work brought him to Russia."

"Was it a social occasion that brought you together, or did you have mutual friends?"

"Really, Mr. Ober. Such personal questions."

"You'll have to excuse me," Ober said sympathetically. "Narrative is my business, and I'm always yearning for more story in real life. Don't you find we live in a world of fragments?"

Mrs. Anderson gave her first smile. "I hadn't thought of it that way."

"In my profession we're constantly evaluating how a story is told and, more often than not, the story that's only being hinted at. Text and subtext, some call it."

"It sounds very rewarding."

"And oftentimes frustrating. Sometimes the fragments are so scant it's hard to know how they go together. For instance"—he produced the engraved compact case—"we found this in Miss Salzman's hotel room, and only this, but these are obviously not her initials." He held the item out for inspection, and Mrs. Anderson took it up, clicking the compact open and shut before handing it back.

"Very strange." Her smooth brow wrinkled. Where at first Ober would've guessed her to be in her early thirties, he saw now that she was a girl in her twenties trying to project an older version of herself.

"I have to ask: Do you know anyone with these initials?"

Mrs. Anderson shook her head.

"It's obviously a special gift from someone. And the lettering tells us about an intimate connection to Russia. And then you're from outside of Moscow."

A glassy look came over Mrs. Anderson. "I've never seen that before."

"The real shame in all of this is that Mr. Swenson must return to California in a day or two, and when he does, the chance for Miss Salzman to return to her new life and employment goes with him. Everything she invested in building that new life will evaporate."

A silence floated between them. Outside, a woman's heels clicked violently against the pavement.

"All right, yes, I know her," Mrs. Anderson said. "Or knew her. That story I told you about meeting my husband in Moscow wasn't true. My husband was looking for a suitable wife, and a marriage was arranged through the international marriage agency I worked for."

Ober had guessed the possibility that Mrs. Anderson was a mail-order bride, but knew she would deny what had become an ugly slur. He nodded in surprise to preserve Mrs. Anderson's dignity in the matter.

"Miss Salzman also worked for the agency, and found a husband in New York as well. The agency is large, as you might know, and we didn't meet until we were here in New York, at one of the monthly dances for the international community."

"Can I presume that her marriage was an unhappy one, if she ended up three thousand miles away under a new identity as a single woman?"

"Quite the opposite," Mrs. Anderson said quickly. "Her husband doted on her. Anything she wanted, she could have. She never heard the word no. Never."

"But then—"

"One day she was just gone. Poof!"

"What did her husband say?"

"He was distraught. He involved the police, who laughed at him and told him she probably went back to Russia. I don't know much, but I know that she didn't return to Russia. She talked very disparagingly about her life there. She found it . . . limiting."

"Perhaps her life in New York was similarly so."

"She never expressed anything like that to me."

"Did her husband know she was returning to New York?"

"I doubt it. He moved back to his hometown after she left. Somewhere in the middle west."

"What was his name?"

Mrs. Anderson twitched. "Henry Williams."

Ober eyed her. "Do you know what she called herself before she became Mrs. Williams?"

"I only knew her as Mrs. Williams."

"And then again as Miss Salzman," Ober reminded her.

Mrs. Anderson stood.

"I'm sorry, but I don't know anything more."

She touched the smooth emerald of the tiny silver necklace that hung around her neck.

"That's very pretty," Ober remarked.

Mrs. Anderson dropped her hand to her side.

"I'd forgotten I was wearing it," Mrs. Anderson said too casually, before reaching for the door.

8

THE MANUSCRIPT MAX HAD BROUGHT ALONG on the hour-long subway trip from Bryant Park to Brighton Beach was less engaging than the one his boss was reading in the seat across from him. He'd noticed a recent trend of first-time novelists rewriting stories of old, giving them a modern twist, which at first Max had appreciated. But the deluge of manuscripts offering retellings had dulled his original excitement for the idea. The bright September morning was too much of a distraction regardless. As the B train hovered on the tracks over Brooklyn, Max found himself lost in the flight. He'd never traveled by airplane and thrilled at the sensation of flying that the BMT line afforded as it shuttled them all the way through Brooklyn, past his own cold-water flat in Brooklyn Heights, to Brighton Beach, the last stop.

The briny smell of the Atlantic Ocean blasted them as they disembarked the train and climbed down from the platform at Brighton Beach Avenue. The sun glinted off the windows of the row houses facing the sea, and the few people moving about did so with such torpidity that it appeared they were walking underwater.

"Did Alexi ever rewrite his book like you suggested?" Max asked.

Ober gripped his hat against a sudden wind and chuckled.

"He claims he's working on it."

Max pulled on the lapels of his jacket. He would need to splurge on a new coat for the winter, which would mean no new books or nights out at the movies for a couple of months.

A man in a straw hat bounded down the boardwalk past them. Max recalled the riots, the year he moved to New York, caused by a group of men who rolled through the city and grabbed straw hats from the heads of unsuspecting wearers and stomped them until they were unwearable. The self-appointed gang was enforcing the randomly decided sartorial rule that straw hats were not to be worn after September 15, but they were soon stomping hats of all kinds. There'd been a ripple of outrage about straw hats as recently as the previous year, when President Coolidge had worn a straw hat on a visit to the city a few days after the so-called deadline. Every time Max spotted a straw hat, he imagined the wearer was daring someone to snatch it from his head. But the man on the boardwalk appeared to have no such bravado about him and was clearly late for something.

The boardwalk was spotted with remnants of multicolored umbrellas erected at the start of the season to welcome the troves of beachgoers piped in from everywhere by the new subway lines, a boon to local business but a source of anxiety among the locals, who cherished their piece of paradise. The Brighton Beach Hotel, a storied destination since it was built by a war profiteer who had poured money into the area, closed shortly after the subway line had been completed, the need for overnight beach accommodations evaporating. The remaining umbrellas were stamped with advertisements from their sponsors, and it was under a faded brown-and-white-striped umbrella emblazoned with an ad for women's reducing soap that Ober spotted Alexi sitting at a rickety table with his backgammon board at the ready.

"Aha!" Alexi cried, his wide, wooden face breaking into a smile. "From Madison Avenue to Moscow!" He unfolded his large frame from the chair, gripped Ober's hand, gave a salute to Max, and then sat down again, expanding and compressing like an accordion. The wisps of his black hair blew in the breeze.

"How are you, Alexi?" Ober asked.

"You know, you know. Want a game?"

"Max here knows how to play."

Max glanced at his boss—they both knew he was terrible at games of any kind—and then took a seat.

"You a hustler?" Alexi asked.

"No, sir."

"We'll see. You roll first."

Max rattled the dice cup and rolled a pair of twos.

"Auspicious start," Alexi said, and smiled.

"How are the revisions coming?" Ober asked.

Alexi touched a thick finger to his scalp. "I got it all up here."

"If only we could get it all out on paper."

"No rush, is there? I'm not the next Dostoyevsky."

"Won't know until you write it down."

Max's pieces marched slowly across the board. He hoped the splitting of Alexi's concentration would be to his advantage but realized that Alexi played without hardly looking at the board, as if by muscle memory alone.

"I know a million stories."

"Know any about Russian mail-order brides?"

"Maybe one or two. But I thought you were happily married." He grinned. "Or is it for the boy?"

Ober gave a short laugh. "Any local girls come over as mail-order brides?"

Alexi clicked his pieces deliberately against the board as he moved them.

"Any bride smart enough to get out of the motherland wouldn't come to the American version of it."

Max sensed he was losing the game but wasn't sure how, or what could be done to prevent it.

"All of the brides you see around here are married to Russians," Alexi continued.

"But say one of these brides wanted to get her single sister out of Russia. Any idea who could make that happen?"

Alexi set down his dice cup, frightening a seagull on a nearby bench. The bird rasped loudly and flapped its wings, joining a flotilla of gulls above as they circled the boardwalk.

"You really are terrible at backgammon," he said to Max, who smiled in agreement. He looked up at Ober, then squinted off into the gray distance, toward the silhouettes of Staten Island. "You're asking about the tailor."

"Which tailor?"

Max felt the sand in his shoes as he and Ober trudged down Neptune Avenue to the address Alexi had given them. They both paused at a pushcart bookseller and perused the faded and dusty hardcovers on display. Max was always on the lookout for a funny title he could surprise Lily with, and his eye caught a red hardcover with the title *O What Fun We'll Have! O the Times!* stamped in gold foil. A brief investigation of its pages revealed it to be the memoir of an average citizen who had unwittingly been present at many seminal events in recent history. But with the purchase of a new winter coat looming, Max replaced the volume among the other treasures awaiting discovery.

Adam & Eva's Tailor Shop was a cramped ground-level space unheralded by any signage, though through the dusty windows one could see the tiny shop overcrowded with bolts of fabric and a couple of ancient sewing machines. A bell rang when they entered, the breeze fluttering the pages of a calendar tacked up on the wall next to the front counter. Ober called out a greeting, but there was no answer. He studied the calendar, which was compliments of Boucher Brothers, one of the bigger printers in Manhattan. All of the lights were turned off, and just as Max was about to suggest the shop was closed, a forceful-looking man with graying black hair appeared with a quizzical look on his face.

"Yes?"

"You forgot to change your calendar," Ober said politely.

The tailor trained his eyes on the calendar, which was still showing August, though he made no move to correct it.

"Can I help you gentlemen?"

"Are you Adam?"

"There's no Adam."

Max accidentally bumped one of the sewing machines and it gave a clacking sound.

"Don't touch that, please," the tailor said. "What do you want?"

"Right to the point," Ober said. "I'm not here for your tailoring services, but I am interested in the other thing."

The tailor trained his cruel black eyes on Ober.

"What other thing?"

"I'm looking for a wife."

The tailor straightened his back and placed his hands on the counter. The knobby knuckles betrayed his years in service of his trade.

"This is a tailor's shop."

"Yes, but I understand you can help."

"He your son?"

Max looked up in surprise.

"No, no. He's my associate."

The tailor scratched the back of his neck slowly.

"Who told you I could help with such a problem?"

"A friend of a friend."

The tailor did not like the evasion.

"Your friend of a friend is mistaken."

"I'm truly sorry to hear that. Perhaps he meant another tailor."

"I don't know any tailors who could help with your particular situation. Besides, he wouldn't be a tailor then, would he? He'd be a pimp."

"Those are your words, not mine," Ober assured him.

The pretzel Max had inhaled on the platform in Brooklyn had done nothing to quell the riotous hunger he felt in the pit of his stomach, and he was dreaming of a cheeseburger from Knox Burgers, a greasy spoon around the corner from the office, when Ober informed him that they'd be transferring at Canal Street and heading south, to Battery Park.

"What's in Battery Park?" Max asked over the rattling of the train.

"Did you notice that the calendar and the notepads and the pens on the counter at Adam & Eva's were all from the same printer?"

Max shook his head no. He hadn't noticed and didn't understand why it mattered.

"What does a tailor need with so much printing?"

Boucher Brothers printshop was nestled at the end of a blind alley. An acrid chemical smell permeated the building, and the pounding of the presses behind a cement wall created an odd cadence to their conversation with the printer, a big, untidy man whose sleepy face was marred by a tiny scar along his jawline. Ober flipped through a stack of catalogs the printer had produced upon request.

"The color in these are excellent."

"Are you looking to print in full color?" the printer asked hopefully.

"I think we'd have to, yes."

"Do you have any more samples?" Max asked impertinently. His hunger had multiplied, and he thought he'd spotted a deli before Ober turned them down the blind alley.

"I think what my associate is trying to say is, well . . ." Ober lowered his voice. "Do you have any photographic collections?"

The printer raised his thin eyebrows, catching Ober's meaning. His face clouded with distrust, however.

"Are you coppers? I don't need trouble from coppers."

"We are not with the police," Ober assured him.

The printer slid open the top drawer of the filing cabinet in the corner and produced a calendar, each month featuring a scantily clad woman in a semiscandalous pose.

"Is this what you're looking for?"

Ober closed the calendar without looking through it.

"Not a calendar, but a catalog. Like a magazine."

The embarrassed printer pawed at the calendar, quickly sliding it into an unseen drawer under the counter.

"We're not in the magazine business, sorry."

Ober tipped the brim of his hat. "I thank you for your time."

The color returned to the printer's face. "I'm sorry we couldn't be of service."

"It's a very particular thing we're looking for. We came expecting to be disappointed."

The thunder from the printing presses drowned Ober out as they turned to leave. The intermediate silence returned, and he said to the printer, "My associate needs to use your restroom. Would you mind?"

What Max needed was a corned beef on rye with extra mustard, but he exchanged glances with his boss and disappeared down the hall indicated by the printer.

A bare bulb lit the cement bathroom, which apparently doubled as a storage room for half-used cans of ink, rolls of newsprint, and a jumble of various cleaners. A dingy mop rested in a rusted pail in the corner. The mirror above the yellow-stained porcelain sink was cracked from side to side.

Max spied the stack of magazines on the back of the toilet and fanned through them. Ober's instincts were rewarded when Max happened upon a catalog filled with black-and-white photos of Russian girls. Each photo had a caption with the girl's name and vital information, including age, hometown, and measurements. Max shoved the catalog down his pants and flushed the toilet for verisimilitude.

9

"GOOD AFTERNOON, MR. OBER," the hall man at the Century Club greeted him. "Your guest is waiting."

Ober fetched Swenson from the Strangers' Room and together they mounted the grand marble staircase, ascending above gilt-framed works by Homer and Sargent to the mezzanine. They perused the lunch menu and sent their order with a whoosh through the pneumatic tube, then strolled through the art gallery while Swenson quietly made an offer for Frederick Orin Bartlett's novel *The Wall Street Girl*. Bartlett's previous novel, *The Triflers*, had been made into a successful movie, and Swenson believed *The Wall Street Girl* could be too. Swenson kept his voice low, knowing the club's policy against discussing business openly. Ober happily accepted the offer on Bartlett's behalf, and together he and Swenson mounted the staircase again. Three right turns brought them to the Birdcage, the dining room overlooking West Forty-Third Street that was decorated with light-colored rugs and white high-back chairs clustered around circular tables fashioned from blond wood.

"You never really know about a person, am I right?" Swenson said when Ober relayed his visit with Mrs. Anderson. "I had no hint of any of this."

"By design, clearly."

The waiter appeared and lunch was served with the customary

efficiency club waiters were known for. The waiter retreated as silently as he'd arrived, another trait prized by the club's well-heeled members.

"What can you tell me about Miss Salzman?"

"I didn't really get a chance to know her well, unfortunately," Swenson answered truthfully. "A typical employer-employee relationship. She seemed to get on well with the other secretaries at the firm. Very independent spirit, from what I could see."

"Any hint of trouble in her personal life?"

"She didn't seem to have one."

"No one came around for her? Lunch dates or picking her up after work?"

"Not that I saw."

"How did she arrive to work?"

"She rode the bus. Many of the secretaries do."

"How was her work?"

"Spotless. Very detail oriented. Unlike my previous girl. Secretarial work is much like waitressing, in my opinion. Everyone thinks they can do it, but few are very good at it."

"It's almost as if she moved to Los Angeles and cast herself in the role of a secretary who lived a quiet life," Ober mused.

"There was one thing that was out of the ordinary," Swenson said. "Most unmarried secretaries live in downtown apartments and have a roommate, maybe two. But she lived in one of those hotels where women land when they come to Hollywood wanting to be in pictures. They're terrible places, usually four and five girls to a room. No privacy whatsoever."

"Did she ever indicate why she lived there?"

"It felt intrusive to ask."

Ober sipped his coffee. "Something about her move to Los Angeles has been nagging at me. It's expensive to travel all the way across the country, and to do so without the promise of a job seems like foolishness, unless you're running away from something. Which is one thing. But the overriding question has to be: Where did she get the money for such a move? Though it seems like she had only enough money to get there, and little else."

"As you might expect, our pay is at industry standard, but it isn't a tremendous amount of money," Swenson added.

Ober discreetly produced the catalog from Boucher Brothers.

"Recognize anyone in these pages?" he asked.

Swenson scanned the black-and white-headshots. "Why, it's incredible." He tapped a picture of a clever-looking girl with dark features and a sarcastic smile. "That's her."

"Vera Rosovsky," Ober said.

"Why call herself Vera Salzman, then?"

"The answer to that question would tell us quite a bit," Ober agreed.

"Is it possible she had a change of heart? Rejoined her old life? She might've been meeting her jilted husband instead of a friend."

"But then why did Mrs. Anderson travel all the way uptown to see her? Wilson said she seemed genuinely surprised not to find Miss Salzman in."

"The friend doesn't seem to have been of much help."

"She didn't claim to be a friend. Only an acquaintance. But I wonder."

Ober flipped the pages of the catalog to the photo of Mrs. Anderson, the former Marina Antipova.

"They're from the same town," Swenson said in amazement. "Look. Ivanovo."

He showed the two pages to Ober. "Remarkable."

"That's not the remarkable part," Ober said. "Most of the girls in this catalog come from the same two or three towns, I noticed. What's interesting is that Mrs. Anderson claimed they met through the marriage service. And that she knew her only by her married name, Mrs. Williams."

"Why would she lie about that?" Swenson asked.

"Perhaps there's a personal animus between the two. Maybe they were rivals of some kind back in Russia. It could be anything, really. A past slight, a shared history they're trying to forget."

"So Miss Salzman's moving to California was to Mrs. Anderson's benefit."

"Could be."

"And what of the compact we discovered?"

"If it's not directly related, it's suggestive."

"It could have been left behind by another guest." Swenson took a bite of his club sandwich and chewed thoughtfully.

"But then we have the coincidence of two Russian women staying in the same room at the same hotel in short order. Life is full of coincidences, but as I'm always reminding my authors, coincidences are in reality fewer and farther between than people believe. What is possible and what is probable are two completely different things."

Swenson laughed. "Too true."

A stocky young man dressed in tweed, with fiery red hair, appeared at their table.

"Good afternoon, Mr. Ober."

"Good afternoon, Bentley. Do you know Peter Swenson, the film agent?"

Bentley extended his hand.

"Robert Bentley, *New York Observer.*"

"I would ask you to join us," Ober said, "but you know the club policy against more than two lunch guests per table."

"I'm on my way out, actually," Bentley said. "I just wanted to see if you've had a chance to read my proposal yet."

"I have, yes." Ober turned to Swenson. "Mr. Bentley has a very interesting idea for a book that might make a terrific film."

"Oh yes?"

"I'll let him tell it."

Bentley assumed his reportorial demeanor. "You've heard of Daddy and Peaches?"

Swenson's knowledge about the millionaire in his fifties who took a child bride earlier in the year had exploded tenfold during his week in New York, thanks to the local papers, which were only too happy to report all the salacious details.

Bentley rattled on. "My idea is to reverse the story, to have a young, wealthy socialite fall for an ordinary boy who lives at home with his mother."

Ober smiled into his soup as Swenson struggled for a response.

"A real head turner, am I right?" Bentley asked eagerly.

Swenson cleared his throat and said judiciously: "It would make people stop and think, I agree."

Bentley smiled proudly. "That's what I'm going for. The effect of the opposite idea. People are crazy for that kind of thing."

"I've actually got a story for you," Ober said. He relayed the details of Miss Salzman's disappearance while Bentley scratched some notes into his reporter's pad. He instinctively omitted the information about Mrs. Anderson and about the jilted husband.

"Straight missing persons, eh?" Bentley said. "Have the police been called?"

"It's only been a couple of days," Ober said. "It won't be of interest to the police yet."

"I'll write it up as a 'Have You Seen This Woman?' piece. Readers love the idea of an amnesiac wandering the streets of New York. Any photo?"

"Afraid not," Swenson said. He pushed his plate with the half-eaten club sandwich away and took up his cooling coffee.

"I'll have the photo guys blur a photo from the archives so you can't really tell who it is. The details are more important anyway."

"Could you refrain from naming the Byrne Hotel?" Ober asked. "I'm sure they wouldn't like the publicity, and it is a clean hotel with a good reputation."

"'Midtown hotel,'" Bentley said as he wrote the phrase down.

"Anyone with information should contact Box 216," Ober dictated.

"Reward?"

Ober shook his head.

"Good secretaries *are* hard to find," Swenson chimed in.

"What's it worth in real dollars?" Bentley asked, his pencil poised.

"Oh, no, no," Swenson said, embarrassed. "I didn't mean . . . well, the firm would frown on that sort of thing anyway."

Bentley promised a piece in the evening edition and bid them luck in their search.

"You think anything will come of it?" Swenson asked after Bentley had gone.

Ober sipped his coffee. "There's no real information to go on, but you never know. The papers are the only way to disseminate the information widely."

"Why didn't you tell him about the mail-order bride angle, or the jilted husband?"

"We're not that desperate yet. She may show up at her hotel tomorrow with an extraordinary story, a real New York tale, and I doubt she'd be thrilled to have her personal biography in the newspaper. Also, we should suppose for the moment that this jilted husband doesn't know about her return to the city. It wouldn't be prudent to expose that fact."

Swenson turned his head in the direction of a car horn out the window. "It's only sinking in now that I may never see her again. One never really gets to know his secretary. I suppose that's not unusual, but this whole baffling case is muted by the realization that she was working and living in Los Angeles under an assumed name."

"We mustn't judge her on that account," Ober said. "We don't have a full grasp of the circumstances. And may never."

"I suppose you're right."

Swenson emptied his coffee cup and stood.

"My last meeting is down the street, at the Algonquin Hotel. Fancy a stroll?"

"I haven't been to the office yet today," Ober said. "I should make an appearance."

Forty-Third Street was bustling with afternoon traffic as they parted.

"If a miracle occurs, I'd like to know about it," Swenson said. "My train leaves in the morning. By the time I reach the coast, the secretarial pool will have sent someone new, I'm afraid. Such is the way these things go."

"Let's hope lost employment is the most devastating aspect of her disappearance," Ober remarked grimly.

10

MAX DESCENDED THE STAIRS of the cast-iron subway entrance on Broadway, slightly out of breath. The marquee at the new Paramount Theatre, slated to open in November, advertised that Thomas Edison was to be a guest at the first showing of *God Gave Me Twenty Cents*, and Max idly wondered if Lily would be interested, if he could get tickets. The buzz around the new theater was immense, and rumors of a massive organ being built by the Wurlitzer company to accompany the silent film only whetted the collective appetites of moviegoers. He put the notion out of his mind just as quickly, focusing on the task at hand.

He'd concocted the ruse when Jim Fayette appeared without an appointment to see Miss Doling. As the receptionist had left sick, Max was working the switchboard, leafing through the new *Vanity Fair*, when Fayette pushed through the door. Rumor around the office was that he was suffering from a severe case of writer's block, an affliction that usually resulted in increased letters and phone calls from Ober's clients. Rare was the occasion when an author simply materialized as Fayette did. He was a thin young man with a fair mustache who smiled at everything, a mask of frivolity guarding an anxious personality, or so Max had learned from Miss Doling. Miss Doling's office was within earshot of the receptionist, though Max could only decipher the strained pitch of Fayette's voice. When he emerged from their meeting, Max blurted out that Fayette's druggist had left a message that he wanted to see him. Almost at the same moment as the lie tumbled from his lips, Max recognized how improbable the message was, that a druggist would track an author down at his literary agent's office, but the puzzled look on Fayette's face, coupled with an awkward exhalation, was the only response, and he bid Miss Doling and Max good-bye.

As it was near enough the end of the workday, and his boss had taken the early train home to Connecticut, Max donned his worn canvas jacket and shouldered his messenger bag, calling out to Miss Doling, who asked him to lock the door on his way out. The elevator closed as Max locked the office door, and he raced down the stairs to beat Fayette to the lobby. Fayette didn't notice him loitering on the sidewalk near the entrance. Max trailed him at a distance as he crossed Madison Avenue toward Fifth Avenue. Fayette unexpectedly ducked into the main entrance of Saks Fifth Avenue, and Max followed. Wilson had warned him about the importance of following suspects in and out of buildings. On his only previous tail job, Max had waited for his mark to exit a bank he'd followed her to, not realizing that the bank had a side street exit as well. So Max kept Fayette in sight. Fayette wandered among the men's shoes, and so did Max. Fayette scanned the bright counter of aftershaves and cologne, and so did Max, careful to remain out of Fayette's peripheral vision.

Then, as if someone had pulled a string, Fayette walked at a rapid clip toward the exit, down Fifth Avenue, and into the heart of Times Square. Max plunged down the stairs just as the green metal subway trolley rattled loudly to a stop. Fayette pushed his way into a crowded car, and Max held on to a strap under an advertisement declaring that Life Savers candies now came in orange, lemon, and lime and inexplicably had a hole punched in the center. The train rocked as it burrowed south. Fayette buried his nose in a copy of the *New Yorker*, and Max settled in for a long ride. Max remembered Lily repeating the conversation she'd eavesdropped on at Scribner between Fayette and his friend about a druggist on the Lower East Side, so he wasn't surprised when Fayette disembarked at Canal Street. The skylights in the Canal Street station let in the dying sunlight, casting shadows against the glazed-tile walls.

Fayette sauntered casually down Canal Street, apparently in no hurry. A large, frazzled businessman with his raincoat flapping open accidentally swung his briefcase into Fayette's knee, and Max ducked into a doorway as the men exchanged words, the businessman rushing past with a look of permanent annoyance on his face. Fayette limped momentarily until he gained his leg again. Max watched until Fayette was under full power, and continued his chase. Max's sense of direction below Fourteenth Street was a source of mirth around the office, and with Wilson especially, who kidded Max about being a lost tourist any time Max tried to give directions to clients. He understood well the grid above Fourteenth, but the streets formed long ago by horse and cow trails confused him, and he could never remember the order of named streets, or if they ran north–south or east–west. Canal ran parallel to Fourteenth, he knew from the map on the wall of the subway car, but as he passed first Mulberry and then Mott Street, he couldn't guess what was next. Fayette abruptly turned down a street called Elizabeth, and Max nearly ran into him as Fayette stood flexing his leg on the steps of an address boasting an orange-and-blue hand-carved wooden sign that read, CITY DRUGS, W. D. EDMONDS, DRUGGIST.

Max froze when he heard Fayette say, "I told you not to bother me."

A big, square-faced man in a white smock appeared at the top of the steps and glanced at Max, who instinctively looked away, staring instead into the clouded windows of the bakery next door.

"You're the one on my steps," Edmonds said in a low baritone.

"I didn't appreciate your little stunt today."

"What stunt was that?"

The men waited for two girls in matching blue-and-green plaid skirts to pass.

"Calling around town looking for me."

Edmonds crossed his enormous arms. "You're getting paranoid."

"Look, I paid this month, so I don't want to be bothered by you or whoever you get to replace that gorilla of yours, may he rest in peace."

"It's bad luck to speak ill of the dead."

Fayette's voice rose in pitch as he said, "It should've been you they threw off that roof."

Edmonds smirked and went back inside.

Fayette massaged his knee and looked up at the sky.

In the distance, a barking dog enticed another high up in a window to respond.

11

SERGEANT ROOSEVELT AND OBER walked silently through the stone quadrangle of Bellevue Hospital, their footsteps echoing like gunfire. The verandas above were dotted here and there with men in white T-shirts sitting in wooden chairs, staring toward the East River. Ober followed Sergeant Roosevelt's hulking figure through an archway and then up a flight of stairs toward the chief medical examiner's office.

"What time was she found?" Ober asked. The empty hallway amplified his otherwise quiet voice.

"Early this morning. The picture in the paper was too blurry to tell for sure, and when you see her face, well . . . But I recognized your post office box address. Anything I can do, you know. I'm in your debt."

Ober recalled the first awkward days years ago when Roosevelt viewed skeptically his offer to pass through information sought by the rest of the police about the crime plaguing the city. But Ober had been true to his word and felt a certain sense of justice in seeing any acclaim diverted from his own clandestine investigations to Sergeant Roosevelt.

"No debts between friends."

Sergeant Roosevelt's mouth turned up, mimicking the big, friendly smile Ober remembered from the early days of Roosevelt's police career. But the quiet backlash and daily torments Ober guessed Roosevelt had to suffer as the city's first black police officer had dimmed and then extinguished his old personality. Gone was the laugh like a cannon shot and the aggressive handshakes and pats on the back. Roosevelt had replaced the earlier version of himself with the quiet, cautious, and self-deprecating simulacrum necessary to do his job among the predominantly Irish and Italian police force. He never spoke of shouldering a heavy burden, but Ober could feel the nameless, faceless specter that haunted Roosevelt. Even though it had been fifteen years since the mayor sued to stop Roosevelt from taking the civil exam, the story was alive in everyone's minds.

The young clerk with wire spectacles too large for his rectangular face nodded as they entered. "Hello, Big Sam."

"The chief here?" Roosevelt asked. He leaned on the counter, and the pack of muscle under his uniform shifted.

"Gone to New Jersey to assist on that Standard Oil thing. All their employees are jumping out of the windows. Locals call it the 'looney gas building.'"

Sergeant Roosevelt was incurious about the goings-on in New Jersey. Ober guessed that Roosevelt had heard all manner of strange occurrences over the years.

"We're going to take a quick look at this morning's Jane Doe."

The clerk pushed his glasses back up the bridge of his thin nose and gave a doubtful look.

"Chief said not to disturb that one."

Roosevelt swung the low gate attached to the counter and held it for Ober to pass. "We're not gonna disturb it."

The clerk looked on helplessly and then returned to the paperwork in front of him.

The lemony smell of antiseptic filled Ober's nose as Roosevelt yanked the handle to the cold storage. Ober stood back as Roosevelt searched the trays until he found what he was looking for. He felt a chill from the room's refrigeration unit and rubbed his arm.

"Here," Roosevelt said. Ober could feel the grinding sound of metal on metal in his back teeth as the body came into view.

Ober peered down at the lifeless body covered in a sheet up to her neck, which had a deep purple ring around it, as did the eyes. The nose was similarly colored and clearly broken. That it was a woman was evident only from the fashionable haircut.

"She got worked over pretty good."

"Where was she found?"

"That's the trouble," Roosevelt said. "She was dumped on the steps of Dilly's, Carmine Russo's blind pig over on Third Avenue, for the morning rush hour to see."

Ober knew the speakeasy Roosevelt was referring to. He had several clients who had, over the years, tried to entice him into joining them on their afternoon lunches at Dilly's. At Scott Fitzgerald's request, he'd loaned John O'Hara the money to settle an overdue bar bill, which O'Hara repaid from the sale of one of his Gibbsville stories to the *New Yorker*.

"Is this the woman you're looking for?"

Ober opened the mail-order catalog to the picture of Vera Rosovsky. The violence had rent her face of the vivacity in the photo, but her features matched. Ober felt a shock of electricity up his spine as he considered the before and after.

"Could I see her personal effects?"

"She didn't have any."

"No jewelry?"

"None."

Roosevelt peered hard into the middle distance.

"No clothing, either."

"You mean she was dumped nude on the sidewalk?"

Ober gave a look of pity to Vera Rosovsky's corpse.

"It's very unusual," Ober continued.

"Not if you take into account that Dilly's is a cop hangout."

A cold silence fell, and for a moment neither said anything.

"Do you think the police stripped the body?"

Roosevelt shrugged.

"Whoever did this knew her intimately," he said. "I've seen plenty of random murders, and this was deliberate and exacting. There's a meaning behind it."

12

UNLIKE SOME OF THE SPEAKEASIES in midtown, which were barely an empty room, some benches, a table, and a few bottles, Dilly's boasted a pressed tin ceiling, cozy velvet couches, and gilt mirrors strung here and there along the redbrick walls. The long room was lit mostly by low lamps, supplemented by candlelight flickering from the firebox of the otherwise unused fireplace along one of the walls that someone had painted black. A carnival of smoke and laughter rose as Ober scanned the room for his lunch companion, Brisbin Norton, one of the less reputable literary agents in town. In the past, he'd successfully declined Norton's invitations based solely on Norton's reputation for cocktail-fueled lunches that quickly turned into dinners that ended late into the evening, but Norton's insistence on meeting was secondary to Ober's curiosity about Dilly's and its proprietor. He'd stood for a moment on the stone steps leading up to the unmarked address and had braced himself for whatever he would have to suffer inside. Miss Salzman deserved justice, and with Swenson en route back to Los Angeles, and the police's silence purchased for a round of free drinks, Ober knew the price for real justice was accepting Norton's lunch invitation, and he was prepared to pay it.

Ober heard his name shouted through the din and spotted Norton on the sole yellow leather couch in the sea of velvet. The chaos of Norton's personality was neatly packaged in the guise of a handsome, fair-haired man with finely cut features. His coal-black eyes burned under a most magnificent pair of eyebrows. Norton extended his hand, and Ober could see his nails had been freshly manicured. He'd slung the jacket of his tailored navy suit over the arm of the couch, revealing a crisp white shirt without suspenders.

"I never thought I'd see Harold Ober in Dilly's," Norton said, smiling. A near-empty highball glass sat before him on a beveled glass table. "Sit, sit."

"I see our meeting has already begun," Ober said, indicating the drink.

He landed in one of the velvet lounges across from Norton and was immediately made uncomfortable by the angle of repose. The murmur of conversation eddied around them as he shifted in his seat.

"That's my assistant," Norton laughed.

Norton ordered another highball from the sprightly waitress with the kind face, most likely her armor against the solicitations of Dilly's patrons, and Ober ordered a soda with a slice of lemon.

"Exotic drink!" Norton guffawed.

Ober let the remark pass and it died in the din.

"You said you had an interesting proposal for me," Ober said.

Their drinks arrived, and the waitress left with a compliment about her gait.

Norton took a long sip.

"Down to brass tacks, okay." He lowered his voice unnecessarily and asked, "You follow the Schellinger case?"

Ober nodded. The surprise acquittal of Arthur Schellinger on charges that he murdered his girlfriend was fresh ink for the newspapers. The facts had been so heavily against Schellinger: he'd picked the girlfriend up from her boardinghouse on Greenwich Street; one of the other guests in the boardinghouse testified that the girlfriend had confided in her that she and Schellinger were to be married in secret that night; Schellinger and the girlfriend had broken the house rule against intercourse while the boardinghouse owner was upstate taking a cure for fever; the girlfriend's bloated body was found wearing Schellinger's plaid muffler, which he claimed to have loaned her when he walked her home and kissed her good night, forgetting the muffler until he'd returned to his home on Millionaire's Row, where, incidentally, Norton also resided, his having married into the family that founded the International Copper Company. Schellinger had seemed destined for Sing Sing, or at least the tabloid headlines had hinted at such, but he assembled the best team of lawyers in New York, who cleverly shifted the narrative away from what did or didn't happen on the last night of the girlfriend's life to the girlfriend's biography, which was an unfortunately seemly tale of boardinghouse evictions and a string of debts that would make sneak thieves blush. Schellinger's lawyers' closing statement convinced the jury that he had barely known the woman. Ober had seen the photos of the party Schellinger hosted at his Fifth Avenue manse in the papers, most of the jurors in attendance, as well as the city prosecutor. He'd kept private his obsessive interest in the case, though he openly shared in the collective outrage about the verdict. Norton's mentioning the case made his skin tingle.

"I've got a new witness, someone who knows an angle that no one else knows," Norton said, leaning forward. He wrapped his slender hands around his drink. "And I want to find a writer to tell her story."

"A woman?"

Norton winced as if he'd been foiled. "Yes, well."

"Why doesn't she go to the papers?"

"Why shouldn't she get paid for her story?"

"Is that her idea, or yours?"

Norton tilted his chin toward the tin ceiling and then smiled.

"Your reputation for matching writers with projects could be the difference in how it gets told."

Ober considered what Norton was saying and then asked:

"Is the witness's story an alibi for Schellinger or something that proves the defense's theory?"

Norton grinned and arched his considerable eyebrows. "Schellinger is long past needing an alibi."

"Not with the court of public opinion."

"I'm sure Mr. Schellinger is not worried about public opinion."

"Men like Mr. Schellinger are *always* worried about public opinion."

"This is what makes you perfect for this project. You see all the angles, all the motivations."

"And what's your interest?"

"A client has come to me with an interesting story that I think will make a sensational book, and I feel a responsibility to see the matter through."

"All the way through? If it becomes a published book, are you going to hold her hand when the press eviscerates her for trying to capitalize on the poor girl's murder? Or will your own motives prevent you from doing so?"

"Are you asking me if we can coagent the book?"

Ober laughed, causing Norton to laugh uneasily.

"Listen," Norton continued, "I know my reputation. Why do you think I came to you? The Ober reputation is sterling, and mine is . . . well, I've made the best deals I could for my clients."

"Your ability to make deals has never been in question," Ober deadpanned.

Norton held up his hands in mild protest. "No one likes a show-off, okay, I understand," he said self-mockingly. "Can I help it if the press loves me?"

"The feeling among your peers is that it's a mutual love affair."

Norton snorted and rose, swaying slightly, betraying that he'd been at Dilly's since long before the lunch hour. "If you'll excuse me," he said, and trampled the fine black bearskin rug that covered the floor like a bloodstain.

Ober sipped his soda water. He'd spent more hours than he could count turning over the evidence in the Schellinger case, sure each time that the prosecution's narrative of the events leading up to and during the night in question were sound and true. And while he found the behavior of the defense unconscionable, he was sympathetic to the jurors' plight.

And now Norton alleged to be able to move the dial on the story, and in the direction of the innocent murdered girl, whose relations were too poor to travel from Ireland for the trial or even to claim her body. No one but he and Max knew that it was Ober's anonymous donation that had allowed for the girl's body to be cremated and sent on a final voyage home. The want to implicate Schellinger—if not in a legal sense, but in print, for all to see—was powerful and Ober felt its pull physically. He swirled the last of his soda water, the lemon drowning in his glass, and decided that he would refuse Norton's offer without explanation. He had none to offer, after all, other than the general distaste for Norton, which he shared with his colleagues in the industry.

"Is it Mr. Ober?" a voice asked. Carmine Russo, a tall, olive-skinned man with enormous blue eyes, appeared. Russo's creaseless white suit hung from his lean frame, a fresh satin pocket square with pink-and-white paisley peeking from the jacket. "Do you mind if I sit?"

Ober motioned toward the leather couch. When he'd accepted Norton's invitation, he'd hoped for a glimpse of Russo, though he hadn't necessarily expected to speak with him. Norton's jacket was still slung over the side, but there was every real chance that he would not return for it.

"Are you being treated well?"

"Yes, very. Thank you."

"I can get you something stronger."

"I'm a law-abiding citizen, I'm afraid."

Russo judged this comment seriously and then laughed.

"My place is full of criminals, then, is what you're saying."

"Not at all. My counsel is my own. Whether or not I agree with the law of the land, I abide by it."

"Thankfully, others feel differently, or I'd be in the poorhouse."

Russo grinned. He sat forward on the couch and put his elbows on his knees.

"You know, for years I've hoped to bump into you. I'm not much of a reader, but I always read the stories by that fellow Cain, in the *American Mercury*."

Ober, too, had followed with interest the work of James M. Cain and said so now, withholding the information that Cain had come to Ober with the idea of wanting to write a novel about the recent Snyder/Gray case, involving a woman in Queens who murdered her husband after buying him life insurance with a double indemnity clause. It was a curious by-product of his profession that mention of any author, whether he represented that person or not, called to mind the author's work over his or her individual personality.

"What a writer!" Russo went on. "He's into the psychology of his characters. That makes it very interesting for the reader."

Ober nodded in agreement.

Russo got a dreamy look in his eyes. "It almost makes it seem like any man could be a writer. Or at least a storyteller. Even a man like me."

"Oh?" Russo's confession caught Ober by surprise.

"Since I started reading Cain and some other crime writers, I thought, well, that I might as well jot down some ideas of my own. I would love to come to your office to talk about them."

Ober was used to demurring when the offer to pitch him story ideas arose, but in this instance he gave Russo an encouraging look.

"The stories from this place would make a great book, I'll bet. A bestseller!" Russo said.

"I don't doubt it."

"This one time me and Pete Hausler were sitting there by the fireplace"—he indicated the exact spot with a flourish—"and this kid, couldn't've been more than fifteen, pushed through and dropped a live grenade in Pete's lap." Russo slapped his knee, overtaken with hilarity. "No one knew who the kid was or where he'd come from, and Pete is as clueless as they come. He couldn't figure why the kid had done it."

"Did it go off?"

Russo slapped his knee again and barked a short laugh. "Dud. Say, that could be the title. *The Dud*."

Russo called out a drink order to the waitress as she scooted by. "And another soda and lemon for my friend."

Ober glanced in the waitress's direction and saw that the previous waifish waitress had been replaced or supplemented by a more buxom version.

"Someone was mentioning another story," Ober said, taking his opening. "Something about a nude body being left on the steps."

The color drained from Russo's cheeks. "I don't think I know what you're talking about."

Ober had assumed Russo would deny the story, since it had been hushed up so expertly by the police.

"Not to worry. The person who told me also told me that it never happened."

This seem to satisfy Russo.

"Did you know the girl?"

Russo shook his head. "Pure craziness."

"So like the grenade, someone dropped something and ran. No reason, no message."

Russo clearly hadn't made the connection, and Ober could see that he was trying hard not to.

"Yeah, I guess."

The new waitress replaced Ober's drink with a fresh one he knew he wouldn't stay long enough to drink, and when she placed Russo's whiskey neat on the table, a tiny silver necklace with a smooth emerald teardrop matching the necklace worn by Mrs. Anderson swung from around her neck.

"Excuse me, where did you get that necklace?"

The waitress looked from Ober to Russo, who sat stone-faced. Her gaze rested on Ober again, and she smiled earnestly and said, "It was in the lost and found for forever."

"It's very pretty," Ober remarked. "I saw one exactly like it recently."

The waitress touched the delicate necklace just as Mrs. Anderson had, and then was called away by a boisterous group in the corner, which included Norton, who vainly tried to wave Ober over.

13

BENTLEY KNOCKED LIGHTLY, then fell tiredly into a chair across from Ober's desk. Max had grown accustomed to the reporter floating in and out of the office at odd times. He acknowledged Bentley with a nod and returned to his work, yet another version of Scott Fitzgerald's new story.

"It came to the paper directly," Bentley said. He handed Ober an envelope. "As it's addressed to me, I opened it. Sorry."

Ober unfolded the piece of blue writing paper inside, on which was written not a letter but the name J. J. Clarke and an address in Hell's Kitchen. Both *j*'s were dotted, as if they were lowercase.

Bentley exhaled loudly and rubbed his forehead. "I'm on fumes."

"I warned you about those all-night jazz clubs," Ober said.

"I wish. Those two wiseguys who robbed that U.S. Mail truck a few months back were allegedly spotted in Staten Island, and I tagged along while the cops went block to block."

Ober remembered the case because the robbers had made off with more than a million dollars.

"And?"

"Nothing."

"New millionaires probably don't retire to Staten Island," Ober remarked drily.

"But dummies run in the same ruts they were born into."

Max snorted from behind his screen and then covered it with a cough. He resumed his typing.

Ober refolded the slip of paper and slid it back into the envelope. He opened the top drawer of his desk and tucked it away.

"What do you think it is?" Bentley asked, yawning.

"Hard to tell. The use of initials is interesting."

"How so?"

"It indicates neither a man nor a woman."

"Clarke is English," Bentley said offhandedly.

"That address makes it more likely Irish."

"Who knows. That part of town is a sewer."

The phone on Max's desk rang and he excused himself.

Bentley sighed. A sudden burst of sunlight through the blinds caused him to squint.

"I'd offer to tag along, but I need some sack time."

"I'll take Max with me," Ober said.

"Boy Friday," Bentley said absently.

"Before you go, have you heard anything about a secret witness in the Schellinger case?"

"Secret witness?"

"Someone is shopping a book claiming to know something about the case. Something that implicates Schellinger."

Bentley's eyes widened. "There was a woman living in the boardinghouse who disappeared the day after the girlfriend was found. They never found her."

"Any details? Age, race, hair color?"

"You can bet she was Anglo," Bentley laughed. "Mrs. Elwell rents to nothing but. After that, zero. Who is shopping the story?"

Ober shook his head. "I can't say for now. Why didn't the woman come up at trial? This is the first I've heard of her existence."

"Cops ruled her out when they couldn't find her. They thought the physical evidence was strong enough, which it was. But it got lost in all the malarkey the defense started pitching about the girlfriend.

At some point, it was hard to remember that someone had been murdered at all!"

"It *was* outrageous," Ober agreed.

"A reporter from the *Herald* got into a fistfight with another from the *Times* when the verdict was handed down." Bentley cracked a smile. "No one jumped in to stop them for at least a good minute."

Bentley slid out to grab an afternoon nap, and Ober tabbed Max for the fifteen-minute walk across Manhattan. As they crossed Eighth Avenue, the transition from midtown to Hell's Kitchen was sudden. The hurried faces of the business class gave way to the stares of the listless and unemployed. It was just past noon, but there was no lunch bustle along West Forty-Fifth Street as Ober and Max approached the address indicated in the anonymous note.

"This it?" Max asked.

A woman bolted suddenly from the ground-floor laundry, and Ober and Max parted quickly to let her pass. The fragrant smell of seasoned meat wafted down from the restaurant on the second floor, adorned with a painted sign that read CHOP SUEY in bloodred lettering.

"The top floor," Ober confirmed.

They mounted the creaky steps with unvarnished treads, the scent of cooked meat growing stronger until they arrived at the third floor, where a scarred door opened when Ober knocked, revealing a two-bedroom railroad apartment with bare floors and walls. A man in painter's overalls with a large, nondescript face and straggly hair of indeterminate color appeared from the kitchen with a mug of coffee in his hand.

"It was open," Ober said.

"Can I help you?" the man asked. He seemed unsurprised to find strangers in his apartment.

On further inspection, Max saw that the coffee mug held a paintbrush soaking in whatever acidic concoction was filling his nose. He sneezed, and the sound echoed through the cavernous apartment.

"My name is Harold Ober, and this is my assistant Max."

"Jaime Clarke," the man said. "Are you here about a painting?"

"We've come on a more urgent matter, I'm afraid. Your name was given in conjunction with a missing person's case."

"Are you with the police?"

"We are not."

Clarke invited them to take a seat at the steel and white Formica kitchen table crammed into the corner. The table was littered with art magazines in both English and other languages.

"How long have you lived here, Mr. Clarke?"

"Since right before the start of the war. The family who owned this entire building lost their only son in 1918 and sold it contingent on the new owner allowing me to stay as long as I like."

"Perhaps you reminded them of their son," Max offered.

Clarke and Ober both gave Max a look, and he retreated into silence.

"Who is missing?" Clarke asked.

"A Miss Salzman."

"That name isn't familiar to me."

Ober reached into his jacket pocket and unrolled the catalog. He showed Clarke the photo of Vera Rosovsky.

"Perhaps you knew her under a different name?"

Clarke stirred the paintbrush in the coffee mug, and the immediate area was suffused with a fresh cloud of chemicals.

"Why the past tense?"

"Excuse me?"

"You said maybe I 'knew' her by that name."

Ober folded his hands in front of him.

"I'm sorry to say the person who is missing is lying on a slab at the county morgue."

Clarke set the mug and brush on the table, his eyes narrowing.

"I know who killed her."

Ober glanced at Max, who remained still in his seat.

"Have you talked to her husband?" Clarke asked.

"We understand that he left New York shortly after she jilted him."

"She was so afraid. She rented a room from me to get away from him."

Ober shuffled his shoes against the hardwood floor in an effort to appear nonthreatening.

"How long did she live here?"

"Just a couple of months. She was on edge the whole time. She ate takeout from the place downstairs almost every meal. She didn't seem to want to go out at all. She called herself Miss Smith."

"A little unusual for a woman to share an apartment with a man who is not her husband," Ober remarked.

"Those are uptown values," Clarke scoffed. "Most of us have to make the best of our circumstances."

"How did she come to rent a room here?"

"I posted an ad at Columbia. I teach there."

"Was she a student at Columbia?"

"She was taking a night course in secretarial work."

"I assume her husband didn't know anything about that, either."

"I doubt it. The words she used to describe him . . . sometimes it made me afraid he'd discover she was staying with me. She said he was a violent man. Would scream at her in Russian, calling her all kinds of crazy names."

"So she never had anyone over?"

"Never."

"How did she pay her rent?"

Clarke scratched an itch on his forearm.

"She paid in cash."

"Was she ever late with payment?"

Clarke shook his head. "Never."

Ober scanned the barren apartment walls.

"And I see you have no phone."

"Chop Suey takes messages for me."

"That's a handy arrangement," Ober said. "When did you last see Miss Smith?"

"She was here until she left for California. A little less than a year ago now."

"Did she alert you that she was coming back to New York?"

Clarke shook his head. "I had no idea."

Max watched his boss appraise whether or not Clarke was telling the truth. Clarke felt the scrutiny and looked away.

"I'd love to see some of your work," Ober said.

The sudden shift in conversation brightened Clarke's disposition.

"I use the spare room as my studio," he said, leading them into the sun-filled room at the other end of the apartment. Finished canvases were stacked five and six deep, leaning against all four walls, leaving a rectangle of standing room where an easel held a new painting. Max could barely make out the contours of a pair of shapely legs, though he guessed it could just as easily be a landscape with a river flowing through it.

Ober browsed through a few canvases.

"If you see something you like," Clarke said, "I'm sure we could come to terms."

"These are all very colorful," Ober said.

The compliment made Clarke beam. "I abhor black-and-white painting," he said.

"And most are portraits," Ober noticed.

"I teach my students that the human form is superior to anything found in nature or, God forbid, in the abstract."

Ober hoisted a canvas up for inspection. Max peered over his shoulder at the painting of a woman in slight repose, her head tipped up, white curtains flowing around her.

"What made you turn this room into a studio, rather than continue to let it after Miss Smith left?"

The question vexed Clarke, and he knit his eyebrows as he struggled for an answer. "I, uh . . . I wanted a home studio. . . . The rent on my studio in the Village was astronomical—"

"Much handier to have a home studio," Ober agreed. "For when inspiration strikes."

"Yes," Clarke said with a touch of relief in his voice.

Ober continued to hunt through the canvases. Outside the clanging bell of a fire truck grew loud and then faded. Max stared at a pigeon perched on the roof of the adjacent building until it flew away.

"Your signature on these paintings has a unique flourish," Ober remarked.

A look of recognition passed across Clarke's face as Ober reached into his jacket pocket and produced the envelope addressed to his post office box. Ober unfolded the slip of paper, and Max could see that the dotted *j*'s matched the artist's signature on all the canvases strewn around the studio.

"I received this tip anonymously," Ober said. "The implication being that you are somehow involved in the disappearance of the woman."

"Someone is trying to frame me!" Clarke protested. A bulbous vein pulsed across his forehead.

Ober refolded the note and handed it to him. He accepted it reluctantly.

"A possibility," Ober said. "But why would anyone want to frame you, Mr. Clarke? And if so, would they really need to forge your handwriting as a part of the frame?"

"Or it could be a prank," Clarke offered in a softer voice. "A student of mine."

Ober gave him a parental look, one Max knew well, and then asked in a casual, friendly tone: "Do you want to tell us why you sent the note?"

Clarke bit his bottom lip and shifted his feet. "I read the item in the newspaper, and even though the picture didn't really look like her, the details matched, and I—"

"So you did know she was in New York?" Ober interjected.

Clarke nodded. "We were going to meet for lunch. She was supposed to call me when she arrived. But she didn't. And then I saw the newspaper and I wanted to make sure you knew about her ex-husband. I'm sure he's responsible!" His voice exploded throughout the studio and he turned, embarrassed. Ober and Max gave him a moment, but he excused himself to use the bathroom. After a moment, it was apparent he wasn't going to return, so they took their leave.

On the landing of the floor below, Ober asked Max if he was hungry, and Max readily accepted the invitation for lunch at Chop Suey, a rich and sweet and oily tang filling his lungs as they were shown to one of the square tables draped with red or white tablecloths. The tablecloths were patterned in such a way that the room took on the look of a checkerboard. Max listened over his wonton soup as Ober reviewed what they'd learned from Jaime Clarke.

"He seems convinced about her husband," Max said, catching a rivulet of soup with his napkin as it rolled down his chin.

"Wilson is looking into the husband," Ober said.

The phone on the wall clanged loudly as their waiter brought their entrees.

"Excuse me," Ober said.

The waiter gave a look of alarm, used to absorbing customer complaints on an almost daily basis, Max guessed.

Ober unfolded the photo of the secretary.

"Do you know this girl?"

The waiter smiled.

"Of course. Miss Smith is one of our best customers!"

The phone rang again, and a large man dressed in white appeared from the kitchen and answered it. He spoke loudly in Chinese and then set the phone on the nearest windowsill.

"When did you see her last?" Ober asked.

The waiter made a step in the direction of the phone.

"Not exactly sure of the day," he said. "Sometime last week?"

14

OBER AND MAX INSTINCTIVELY CROSSED to the sunny side of
Fulton Street to counter the midmorning chill coming off the East
River. Because construction wasn't yet complete on the Second
Avenue subway system, which would've provided a straight shot
from the Ober offices to the South Street Seaport, they'd traversed
the length of Manhattan on the Fifth Avenue bus. The stolid edifice
of the Brooklyn Bridge rose above them, lit on the Brooklyn side
by sunlight, the Manhattan side cast in shadow. For a short time
after moving to New York, Max had been fearful of the spate of
kidnappings at the seaport, men disappearing as they stumbled
home from seaport saloons, presumably kidnapped to work Rum
Row, the illegal pipeline controlled by the Mafia that brought
alcohol into New York. Being safely ensconced in midtown, he'd
largely forgotten the tales of missing persons. Plus, the seaport
was to him as exotic a location as the islands in the Pacific Rim.
But he shuddered as he kept up at Ober's heels. They passed the
beehive of activity inside the Fulton Fish Market and walked two
short blocks south to find the fruit of Wilson's surveillance of
Mrs. Anderson: Decker's Luncheonette, a cramped two-window
operation on the ground floor of a warehouse for the Great Atlantic
Seafood Company. Wilson had at first assumed Decker's was Mrs.
Anderson's lunch spot of choice, but he observed her more than once

in conversation with the tall, sandy-haired proprietor and concluded he was the impetus for her visits.

Decker's was little more than an airless box with a long counter made of indeterminate wood, and metal stools with worn black leather seat cushions. The chalkboard behind the counter advertised oysters, hot dogs, coffee, and cheesecake. The luncheonette smelled strongly of popcorn, though Max couldn't locate the source.

"Not open yet," the sandy-haired man behind the counter said in a slow and apologetic voice as he replenished his supply of paper coffee cups and napkins. He plunged his hand into the sink and rescued a handful of silverware, which he proceeded to dry and separate.

"We're looking for a moment of your time."

Ober took another step toward the counter, and Max followed suit.

"Who's asking?"

Ober gave his name and introduced Max. The sandy-haired man had a cautious air about him, and he suddenly became guarded.

"What do you want?"

"Would a cup of coffee be out of order?" Ober asked. He and Max were standing at the counter, worn smooth from years of service.

"Coffee's not ready yet," was the answer.

"Is there popcorn?" Max asked hopefully.

A blank stare told him otherwise.

"I can offer you some lemonade," the man said.

"Two, please," Ober said, and put a dollar bill on the counter. "Nice place, this. How long have you owned it?"

"A year or so."

A strong wind blowing from the ocean caused the front door to flutter and then come to rest. The sandy-haired man put a glass of lemonade in front of each of them.

"We have an interest in a customer of yours, Mr. . . . ?"

The sandy-haired man appraised Ober and then, deciding something, offered his hand.

"Mr. Kelly."

"A pleasure." Ober shook hands and continued: "We're looking into a matter involving an acquaintance of Mrs. Anderson."

"Police?" Mr. Kelly asked warily.

Ober shook his head.

"How often does Mrs. Anderson lunch here?"

"Now and then."

"Do you have a lot of female customers?" Ober asked in a manner that indicated that he doubted that was the case.

"A few."

"Mrs. Anderson lives on the west side of town," Ober said nonchalantly. "It's curious to me that she travels across the city for your cuisine. No offense meant."

Mr. Kelly shot a piercing look.

"Does she ever dine in with Mr. Anderson?"

Mr. Kelly eyed him. "What's this got to do with Billy?"

"Are you personally acquainted with Mr. Anderson?"

Mr. Kelly cracked a half smile. "You could say that, yeah." He slid a cavalry of salt and pepper shakers across the counter and began unscrewing their caps. "He's my half brother."

Ober tilted his head to one side and smiled. He stroked his long chin in a manner Max had seen a thousand times before and which anticipated a moment of silence while Ober contemplated a new and unexpected piece of information.

"What made you ask if we were with the police?" Ober asked suddenly. "The benign Mrs. Anderson doesn't strike me as so nefarious a character that the police would be calling after her."

Mr. Kelly made a funnel with his thumb and forefinger over a salt shaker and carefully filled it. His lips twitched as he concentrated on the task before him but also, Max thought, with a credible answer to Ober's question.

"I'm actually a literary agent," Ober said. "I represent writers and their interests to publishers."

"Aren't many writers around here," Mr. Kelly said smartly.

Ober laughed. "I've learned that storytellers come in all guises," he said. "I have a client, a Russian émigré who sits on the boardwalk down in Brighton Beach and plays backgammon with strangers all day. He knows more stories than most. In fact, he's working on a book I'm hoping to sell. He wants to use the title 'Durashkas,' but I told him the English translation would be better for the American market. But he thinks 'Sweethearts' is too sentimental. Prefers the hard and soft cadences of the Russian. Which do you think is better?"

"I don't really read books," Mr. Kelly said. "A little of the newspaper and that's about it."

Ober didn't acknowledge the confession, but waited a beat and then asked: "Have the police been around asking about Mrs. Anderson?"

"Not that I know of," Mr. Kelly said.

"Do you have other employees?" Ober asked doubtfully.

Mr. Kelly shook his head as he tackled a half-filled pepper shaker.

"She's not as benign as you might think," he said, smiling.

Max rattled the ice in his empty glass. They were getting nowhere with Mr. Kelly, and he began to think Wilson had mistaken the importance of Mrs. Anderson's visits to her brother-in-law.

"Did you know her friend from back home, Vera Rosovsky?" Ober asked.

Mr. Kelly seemed surprised to hear the name.

"Why are you asking about Vera?"

"So you know her."

"You could say that."

Ober sat contemplating. Max hoped they'd stay long enough to enjoy an early lunch. He was lost in the thought of a dozen fresh oysters when his boss said:

"You were married to Vera, am I right?"

Mr. Kelly quit his busywork and gave Ober a long stare.

"That's right," he said. "What of it?"

"But she left you."

"Again, what of it?" Mr. Kelly's voice acquired a menacing tone.

"And Mrs. Anderson told you Vera was back in New York?" Ober asked.

Max set his glass on the counter, and Mr. Kelly refilled it without being asked.

"No point in denying it," he said. "Since you are intent on pursuing the matter. Yeah, she said Vera had returned to the city. What of it?"

"Did you know she had left New York?"

"I'd heard a rumor."

"From whom?"

Mr. Kelly shrugged. "You'd be surprised the kinds of things that float around a luncheonette."

"Did you know she'd moved to California?"

"Could've been the moon. Doesn't really matter."

"Did she call you with plans to get together?"

"Nope."

"Did you go see her at the Byrne Hotel?"

Mr. Kelly tightened the lids on all the shakers.

"I didn't."

"But you knew which hotel she was staying at?"

"Marina—Mrs. Anderson—told me, sure."

"And you weren't curious to reunite with the woman who had jilted you?"

"Not really. If she wanted to see me, I'm not hard to find. Truthfully, I haven't thought about her much since she left."

"Her wanting to see you is not the same thing as you wanting to see her," Ober said. "The difference isn't really even subtle, with respect."

"Marina wanted me to pay her a visit, is that what you're looking for? She was sure it would make Vera happy, but I wasn't convinced. Marina is a little . . . well, you have to understand. When Billy and I were first married to Marina and Vera, we were quite the foursome. Admittedly, it was great fun. Billy and I grew up in Ohio, so we hardly knew the city when we moved here together to get out of the stink-hole small town our relatives were drowning in. Finding Marina and Vera through the travel service was part of our plan to establish ourselves as respectable New Yorkers."

"But that ended pretty quickly for you," Ober pointed out. "That must've been a sour experience, and a disappointment."

"Mostly for Marina," Mr. Kelly admitted. "That's why she told me about Vera's coming back to New York. I think she secretly hopes that one day the four of us will roam the streets like back in the old days."

"But now it's too late."

Mr. Kelly screwed up his face.

"Why is it too late?"

"I'm sorry to be the bearer of such bad news," Ober said plaintively, "but your wife is dead. She was found beaten to death on a sidewalk in midtown."

Mr. Kelly gazed out the window for a long moment. "I'm sorry to hear that," he said at last. "She really was great fun. Did they catch who did it?"

"The police don't have any leads, I'm afraid," Ober said.

Two seamen pushed noisily through the front door and sequestered themselves at the lone corner table.

"I'm sorry I can't offer you gentlemen any more time," Mr. Kelly said.

Ober stood and Max followed his lead.

"Our condolences for your loss," Ober said with a touch of sarcasm.

Max watched as the jab landed and Mr. Kelly winced.

"Tell the police to look into her mobster boyfriend," he said quickly. "Maybe they'll find some answers there."

"Carmine Russo?"

Mr. Kelly nodded. "Already onto him? Good." He slid the dollar back toward Ober. "On the house," he said, and then came out from behind the counter to serve his first real customers of the day.

15

MAX IMMEDIATELY REGRETTED involving Lily in the scheme. But when he'd asked her to recruit a couple of Dominoes, she'd insisted on coming along.

"Is it dangerous?" she'd asked hopefully when he approached her at the bookstore. Max had assured her it wasn't, but now he wasn't sure he'd spoken the truth.

The plan had been hatched quickly on the walk from the subway to City Drugs. The two Dominoes, Bert and Hank, were mildly disguised with hats pulled down over their shaggy hair. Bert was wearing a pair of spectacles as part of his costume, and Hank had a series of plaid scarves layered around his neck to alter his appearance. Max told them he needed a few minutes alone in the shop to look around, five or ten at the most. Lily had offered to faint on the sidewalk in front of the drugstore, but Max worried that ploy would draw a crowd, which was the opposite reaction he was going for. They decided on the shoplifting ruse based solely on Hank's bragging that he and his brother routinely stole from the five-and-dime around the corner from their place in Queens.

As they approached City Drugs, the sky darkened, which Max took as an ominous sign. But he'd convinced himself that W. D. Edmonds was the centerpiece of the mystery about the disappearance of Jeannette Barnes's boyfriend, though he also had to admit that his lack of other leads had influenced his thinking on the matter.

Edmonds cast a glance in Max's direction as he and Lily entered. Bert and Hank had preceded him and were pretending to browse the aisles of powders and elixirs. Bert coughed loudly as if he were sick, an improvisational touch Max appreciated. He had made no promises of money or anything else to Bert and Hank, and it had quickly become apparent on the walk over that they had readily volunteered in an effort to impress Lily. Max knew that impulse and respected it.

"What are you looking for?" Edmonds's deep voice seemed to shake the windows, though in reality the effect was caused by the shudder and stop of a yellow delivery truck out front. Edmonds came out from behind the counter and propped open the glass door with a red brick kept hidden behind a wooden crate. He waved to the two deliverymen, who set about unloading the truck of its wares.

"Do you sell Squirrel Nut Zippers?" Lily asked.

Edmonds made a face. "There's a candy store down the street, miss."

"Have you tried the new vanilla flavor?" she asked.

A loud crash coming from the direction of the truck drew Edmonds's attention.

Max shook his head at Lily, who stuck her tongue out at him. This impromptu conversation with Edmonds, coupled with the appearance of the delivery truck, made him nervous. Bert and Hank continued to roam the aisles, and Edmonds continued to monitor them, but his attention had been split between them and the delivery. Max edged toward the counter, convinced that whatever he was searching for was hidden in the back room behind the black felt curtain. The curtain had collected a layer of white fuzz from Edmonds's smock and who knows what else. Perhaps he could duck into the back room while Edmonds was dealing with the delivery— the room couldn't be larger than a closet, after all—rendering Bert and Hank's ruse unnecessary.

Edmonds exited the store, his large frame hovering on the top step, watching as the deliverymen reassembled the contents of a box that had spilled out onto the pavement. A skinny man on a secondhand bicycle clanged his bell and waved to Edmonds, but he didn't wave back. Encouraged by a nod from Lily, Max stepped behind the counter, but as he reached to part the curtain, a phone he hadn't previously seen hanging on the wall rang, a peal of bells ringing in his ears, causing him to retreat. The wooden floorboards creaked under Edmonds's weight as he reached for the phone. He eyed Max as he answered and kept his gaze as he grunted through a short conversation and hung up.

"What can I help you with?" Edmonds asked.

Max folded his hands in front of him, a habit he'd groomed for when he wanted to appear innocuous and unmemorable.

"Do you develop photographs?" he asked.

Edmonds squinted, his features darkening. He shook his giant wooden head no. "Used to," he said gruffly. "No money in it."

"Oh," Max said, affecting disappointment. He felt Lily's eyes on him. "Can you recommend anyone? I have some pictures that I . . . well . . ." His voice trailed off into a whisper.

Edmonds scrutinized him and then glanced at Lily, who moved toward the door. He opened his mouth, revealing a cavern of tar-stained teeth, but before he could answer, Bert and Hank bolted from the back of the store, upsetting a display of cough drop boxes, and bounded down the steps. Edmonds thundered after them, almost knocking Lily over as he chased after them. The commotion drew the attention of the deliverymen, and Max accounted for all the players—Lily on the steps, Bert and Hank in the street, Edmonds chasing after them, the deliverymen watching and laughing—before he darted through the curtain. His eyes adjusted in the tiny back room filled with overstock. He realized in horror that he'd been counting on whatever he was looking for to be in plain sight, and that he'd half expected to find a darkroom or other easily identifiable evidence of Edmonds's blackmail scheme. He hadn't anticipated a manual search of anything like a back storage room and was stymied by being unsure of what it was he was supposed to find. He gave up and stepped back out into the light.

In his mind, the tableau outside was frozen in time, so when the packet of yellow envelopes bound by a greasy rubber band under the counter caught his eye, and he swiftly tucked the whole lot into his jacket pocket—each had a name written at the top and what felt like photographs inside—he was surprised to find Edmonds standing over him rather than out in the street with the others. Gone was the delivery truck, and there was no sign of Bert or Hank, or even Lily for that matter. The pharmacy was as ghostly quiet as the stage at a Dominoes production.

"That's my property," Edmonds said patiently.

"I don't know what you mean," Max said, panic rising in his chest. He tried to push past Edmonds, but the druggist caught hold of him and tossed him effortlessly to the floor. Edmonds reached under the counter and the silver glint of a pistol became the focus of Max's attention.

"I'll take back what's mine," Edmonds said, less patiently than before.

Max wanted desperately to jump to his feet, but his legs had gone dead under him. The wood floor was cold to his touch as he hoisted himself up on his elbows. His mind raced back to a time he and Ober had been cornered by a desperate bookkeeper they'd been investigating for embezzlement. Ober had casually taken the gun from the bookkeeper, and later, in answer to Max's question, he'd said that he could see the gun wasn't loaded. But Max could see the dull lead caps of the bullets in Edmonds's gun.

"Who sent you?" Edmonds suddenly demanded. "Hanrahan? That weasel."

"I don't know anyone named Hanrahan," Max said slowly.

"Get up off the floor and give me back my pictures," Edmonds directed.

Max managed to get to his knees, the pistol still trained on him. Edmonds took a step backward, as if Max were about to make a sudden move, and both were startled by the front door opening and closing. Max was further startled to see Miss Doling standing at the counter, wearing the prim but innocent smile of a customer who had wandered in off the street. He wanted to rush over and hug her, but refrained. Edmonds lowered the gun behind the counter.

"Can I help you, miss?" Edmonds asked in an annoyed tone he hoped would shoo her away.

"It's rather embarrassing," Miss Doling said, "but there are two hoodlums I believe are following me, and I'm carrying some cash for my employer. I stopped in to see if they would pass, but they're waiting on the street corner. Would I be able to use your phone to call the police?"

Edmonds replaced the pistol under the counter at the mention of the police, though he nodded at Max in a threatening way, as if to telegraph that they had unfinished business. "The police won't come," Edmonds said, more hopeful than certain.

"I'd be happy to escort you," Max offered.

Edmonds started, but before he could interject, Miss Doling said quickly, "Oh, you're such a dear. That would be wonderful. I've never been so frightened."

"A pleasure, ma'am," Max said.

"You really can't be too careful," Miss Doling went on. "You read about these kinds of things in the newspaper, but you never imagine it'll happen to you."

"Better to be safe," Max agreed.

"I'll be in touch about my property," Edmonds said as Max opened the door for Miss Doling. He hooked his arm in hers as they walked down Canal, passing Bert and Hank, who were loitering on the street corner. Lily sat on a nearby stoop, smoking. Max gave them a wave of thanks, and Lily saluted, the cigarette burning between her fingers.

Max and Miss Doling boarded a trolley just as it lurched uptown. A short man with a round face and a sack of groceries in his lap gave his seat to Miss Doling, and they rode in silence until the next stop, where the woman who was sitting next to Miss Doling and clutching several shopping bags disembarked, and Max sat down.

"Thank you," Max said finally.

"I won't ask," Miss Doling said.

"How did you know?"

"You were acting nervous all day at the office," Miss Doling answered. "You probably made more filing mistakes today than Mr. Ober's last two assistants combined. I was curious about what had you so distracted. And since I was heading this direction anyway to deliver my edits on Josephine Bergin's new manuscript . . ."

Max smiled.

"Was it worth it?" Miss Doling asked. "I mean, were you successful?"

Unsure of what the envelopes in his pocket contained, but possessing an inkling, he simply nodded rather than risk scandalizing Miss Doling.

"Well, then, good," she said.

The trolley bounced along on its tracks, stopping every few feet, it seemed. Max had always hated trolleys and avoided them if at all possible.

"And how goes it in the search for Miss Salzman?" Miss Doling asked after a bit.

Max recounted what he and Ober had learned about Mr. Kelly, including Kelly's insinuation that Carmine Russo might know more than he was letting on, and also about their trip to the apartment in Hell's Kitchen where the secretary had apparently gone to hide out.

"I wonder why she was taking secretarial classes at Columbia?" Max mused.

"She would have to work," Miss Doling said. "After leaving her husband, I mean."

"True," Max agreed. "Maybe I should take a trip up to Columbia," Max said, though it was more of a question.

"I'm sitting in on a writing class at the invitation of an old professor friend of mine," Miss Doling said. "I can ask a couple of questions while I'm there."

The understanding that she would do so on the quiet passed between them, as it had many times before. Miss Doling had, in the past, proved invaluable to their investigations, and Max lamented that she didn't receive her due, but he also sensed that she preferred the arrangement—it may even have accounted for a measure of excitement—and moreover that Miss Doling understood that her employer was only shielding her from the moral code of society, rather than inflicting his own values. Against the prevailing winds, Ober had promoted Miss Doling to his equal in their literary endeavors, a position she relished above all else. But if she could be useful in other ways, she would.

Later, alone in the office, Max slipped the empty envelope with Jim Fayette's name and address on it in the top drawer of Miss Doling's desk, along with a handwritten note that he'd found the envelope in the elevator and that Fayette must've dropped it. She would return the empty envelope to Fayette without comment, and Fayette would know the matter had been resolved in his favor. Max had burned the pictures, along with all the others, in the basement incinerator. He fed the envelopes into the fire too—the names and addresses and Edmonds's greasy fingerprints on everything turning to ash—keeping out only Fayette's and the one with the name and address of Philip Slater. Curiosity had gripped him and he'd peeked at the photos of Slater in various compromising scenes. He set the pictures aflame, relieved that Jeannette Barnes would never know about them. But the sense of dread he'd felt at opening the envelope remained. Philip Slater's address in Yonkers worried him more than the photographs did.

16

"SERGEANT ROOSEVELT ASKS if you could you pay him a visit at your convenience," Max said, leaning in his chair to be seen and heard from behind the wooden screen.

Ober's anonymity at Police Plaza was threatened every time he appeared, but he knew Sergeant Roosevelt understood that, and he'd respected the few times Roosevelt had summoned him. A further complication was the lack of privacy afforded Roosevelt, his metal desk one in a flotilla of metal desks stationed under bare bulbs hung from the basement rafters. The other sergeants on the force had their desks moved out of the bull pen and into the corners, where they were cordoned off by three-quarter paneled screens, but Roosevelt's remained firmly in place and squarely in sight, which was why Roosevelt led them to the records room, the towering wooden filing cabinets standing sentry over their conversation.

"Thanks for coming down," Roosevelt said. He absentmindedly touched a fresh shaving nick on his chin.

"Always enjoy a trip downtown," Ober said, smiling.

Roosevelt leaned against a filing cabinet, which cinched tight against the wall as it absorbed his weight. "The body has been taken," he said.

Ober tossed the newspaper he'd been reading on the train into the wastebasket.

"But what about my tip identifying her?"

"I filed the report, like we said," Roosevelt answered. "But the paperwork is missing. Like it never happened."

Ober hung his head. "What does it mean?" he asked.

Sergeant Roosevelt pursed his lips and said, "My guess is her body will wash up in the river, and the ME will send it to a body farm upstate after a day or two, claiming disfiguration beyond identification."

Ober's indignation produced a bitter bile at the back of his throat. His initial interest in the world of books was owed to his belief that literature could inspire compassion among readers, but lately he'd come to lament that only those already predisposed to compassion were readers. The act of removing the secretary's body violated a hundred different ideals Ober held dear.

"Russo," Roosevelt said.

Ober nodded in agreement. "And yet he denies knowing her."

"He knew her, all right," Roosevelt said. "For a year or so, I've been quietly putting together the pieces of Russo's smuggling empire, mostly information from low-level informants who can't stomach that Russo has amassed such riches on their broken backs."

"How do you know the information isn't just retribution?"

"Sometimes it is," Roosevelt admitted. "It's usually easy to spot because it's so preposterous. Also, there are limits to what men of a certain station can know."

"How low is your source on the girl?"

Roosevelt smiled. "As low as you can go, but he's also related to the primary source. I took a trip to a town outside Albany to look into a warehouse I'd heard about, one of Russo's, but the warehouse was on private property and I couldn't get near it. It was late in the day, so I decided to take a room and head back in the morning. The hotel in town claimed not to have any vacancies"—Roosevelt grimaced, the only hint he ever gave about the oppressive obstacles thrown at him by the white man's world—"but they recommended a room in a house down the road, which I let from a poor family who was grateful for the night's stay. They provided a meal, too, though I understood that it would be served to me in my room." Another grimace. "As I returned my dishes to the kitchen, I surprised what turned out to be their son as he came home. I couldn't tell what shocked him more: a policeman in his mother's kitchen, or a black man," Roosevelt laughed. "But I introduced myself, and the son and I got to talking over a game of gin rummy. I think he thought he could get some money off me."

Ober laughed. "He clearly doesn't know your reputation."

"News from the city travels slowly to those parts," Roosevelt said, grinning. "So we're playing a few hands and he asks me what I'm doing there and I take a gamble and tell him. He sets his cards down, and for a moment I think I've made a mistake, something grave even. Maybe the kid works for Russo, or knows him and will relay the information that I'm sniffing around about him." Roosevelt gave a frank look. "I'm the only officer on the force willing to take Russo on, but if he discovers that fact, he could easily put an end to it, as you know."

"Yes," Ober agreed softly, knowing the implication of what Roosevelt was saying was true.

"So the kid looks me over, like he's deciding whether or not to trust me, and I make myself as agreeable as I can, which, at this point, I'm pretty good at. I compliment his mother's cooking and the cleanliness of the house. You know, soft, soft, soft. But now the kid is curious. He has to know exactly what I'm doing there. He asks me what I want with Russo and I tell him about the warehouse. He asks me if the warehouse is going to be raided, and I assure him it isn't, that I couldn't get anywhere near it."

"Bet he was relieved to hear that," Ober laughed.

"More than I knew at the time. He tells me his cousin works there. 'What sort of work?' I ask, and the son doesn't know specifics, or he doesn't want to say. I let on that I'm not so much interested in the warehouse as I am in Russo himself, an idea so big it seems safe for him to go ahead and tell me that in fact his cousin used to work for Russo directly in the city, but Russo banished him back upstate because he thought the cousin was getting fresh with Russo's girlfriend."

Ober started. "You mean . . . ?"

Roosevelt nodded.

"And that's not even the real story. The cousin *was* friendly with the woman—the son didn't recall her name when I told him, but the descriptions matched—and I asked what eventually happened to the woman, and the son told me that Russo gave her some money and sent her to California to have his child and give it up for adoption. Russo wanted her to come back from Los Angeles when it was all over."

Ober gave a look of surprise. "She didn't look like a woman who had recently given birth," he said.

Roosevelt's eyes twinkled. "She hadn't. I checked with the ME."

"Were there any scars that might mean—"

"Nothing like that, either."

"I've wondered all along how she came up with the money to move across country. She didn't seem to have any regular means of income."

"Pretending to be pregnant by Carmine Russo seems to have bought her a ticket to California."

Ober rubbed his large hand along his jawline. "It's also quite a risk. Either she never planned to return, in which case she chances that Russo will come looking for her, or she intended to return to New York and pretend that she'd given up a child for adoption. We don't know enough about her to know if she possessed such theatrical skills. It's in the realm of possibility, but highly improbable."

"Has your sleuthing turned up anything that might give a hint about what she was up to?"

The door to the records room popped open, and a startled young officer gave a quizzical look.

"He's at lunch," Roosevelt intoned, and the young officer retreated, closing the door behind him.

Ober leaned an elbow atop a near filing cabinet.

"What we know so far is that Miss Salzman came to New York via Russia as a mail-order bride—"

Roosevelt gave a low whistle.

"—and was part of a foursome that included a friend from Russia and two American brothers. Miss Salzman's friend is still married and lives on Vesey Street, a Mrs. Anderson, while the jilted husband of Miss Salzman owns and operates Decker's Luncheonette down at the seaport."

"You got all of that from Mrs. Anderson?"

"None of it. In fact, Mrs. Anderson took great pains to conceal the true nature of her relationship with Miss Salzman. Her apartment is devoid of any keepsakes or photographs that aren't very recent. She even lied about the fact that her brother-in-law was the jilted husband."

"But why would she lie about that?"

"Perhaps to protect the brother-in-law."

Roosevelt nodded. "Do you think she believes the jilted husband killed her?"

"She may," Ober said slowly. "The jilted husband—Mr. Kelly is his name—pointed the finger at Carmine Russo, so he's aware of the fact that she was dating Russo."

"Maybe he killed her and dumped her on Russo's doorstep to make a statement. For revenge."

"A possibility. Kelly *was* pretty collected when I told him that his ex-wife had been found dead. Most men would've reacted with some emotion, regardless of the circumstances of their marriage." Ober tapped his fingers along the top of the filing cabinet. "I got the feeling that the marriage simply didn't work out. Perhaps Kelly felt pressured into the marriage by his half brother—Kelly said that he and his brother had moved to New York from Ohio to start their adult lives, and maybe the double marriage seemed like a step in that direction. But then maybe Kelly realized it wasn't a good match and wanted to get out of it. But the testimony of the artist in Hell's Kitchen, J. J. Clarke, seems to contradict that notion. She told Clarke she was deathly afraid of her husband. But she also told him that her ex-husband would yell at her in Russian. I played a little trick on Mr. Kelly, I'm ashamed to say. I told him about a supposed manuscript I was reading with the Russian title '*Durashkas*,' which means 'idiots,' but I translated the title as 'Sweethearts' and he didn't correct me."

"So he doesn't speak a word of Russian."

"Yet she used the name Miss Smith in Hell's Kitchen, which means she was afraid of something."

"Maybe it was really Russo she was hiding from," Roosevelt offered. "Maybe she used the story of the jilted husband as a ruse to avoid mentioning Russo. Anyone would be less likely to rent a room to someone on the run from someone like Russo."

Ober nodded thoughtfully. "The artist certainly would've been spooked by mention of Russo. He seems to lead a quiet if timid life."

Roosevelt shifted from one leg to the other. "Do you want me to pay the artist a visit? I could suggest Russo is involved, to see if he's holding anything back."

Ober smiled. "You might give him a heart attack."

A tidy man in a tight-fitting suit was surprised to discover Roosevelt and Ober among the filing cabinets.

"Can I help you gentlemen?" the records keeper asked as he dropped a brown paper bag on his desk.

"Just having a chat," Roosevelt said.

"I'm very busy," the records keeper said brusquely.

Ober followed Roosevelt into the hall.

"One of the waiters at the restaurant below the apartment in Hell's Kitchen claims to have seen Miss Salzman recently. The apartment doesn't have a phone, and the restaurant took messages for the artist and Miss Smith, as she was called there. But it might've been confusion on the waiter's part. The artist said he was supposed to meet her for lunch, but that she didn't contact him when she got to New York."

"Waiters are notoriously unreliable witnesses," Roosevelt said. "The monotonous nature of their work leads them to sometimes mistake one day for the next."

Ober smiled and shrugged. "The real question that's been nagging at me during all of this is: Who posed as Miss Salzman's brother at the Byrne Hotel?"

"Could the staff give a description?"

"Apparently, there was a plumbing emergency that morning, and the staff was so discombobulated they couldn't really even give an accurate description of any of the plumbers who arrived on scene to help."

"As unreliable as waiters," Roosevelt chuckled.

On his way out of Police Plaza, Ober happened upon Bentley in the stone courtyard, feeding the last of a bagel to a gaggle of pigeons. Another reporter Ober didn't recognize waved to Bentley, and Bentley waved back.

"If you feed them, they keep returning," Ober said.

Bentley smiled.

"Pigeons inside and out," he said, laughing.

The smallest pigeon in the scrum edged forward and snapped the piece of bread from between his fingers, startling Bentley, who stood and tossed the rest of the lumpy bagel into a nearby bush. The pigeons descended on it mercilessly.

"Did anything more come of the piece about the missing woman?"

"Yes, thank you for your help. As always."

"Glad to be of service. You found her?"

"We did."

"Anything I can know about? For the record?"

Ober shook his head. "It's still all a bit muddled, I'm afraid."

"Let me know first, though, will you? When you untangle it."

"Of course."

"I was actually going to drop in on you when I was next your way."

"Oh?"

Bentley glanced over his shoulder and squared to face Ober. He lowered his voice.

"Schellinger knows about the secret witness. And he's eager to find out who she is. And where she is."

17

MISS DOLING SAT DUTIFULLY in the vaulted marble rotunda of Low Memorial Library and listened to students in her friend Professor O'Hara's creative writing class critique one another's work. The Ionic columns were the least ornate feature of the library. Miss Doling couldn't make out the meaning of the looping ironwork atop the octagonal bookcase around which the tables were arranged. A statue of a bronze eagle spreading its wings for flight perched on the four-faced clock, whose hands moved interminably slow. When prompted, Miss Doling offered her own comments on the student work she'd perused on the subway ride over, but her mind was preoccupied with thoughts about Swenson's secretary. She admired Miss Salzman's wanting to improve her standing by subscribing to secretarial classes at Columbia. Miss Doling herself had no such training. She was lucky that a job answering phones for *Collier's* had led to reading and evaluating manuscripts for the magazine's editor, who continually bragged about her to the authors and agents that frequented the halls of *Collier's*. But while her literary tastes were valued, which was a source of pride, she never rose in the ranks above that of an editorial assistant. So when Mr. Ober mentioned that he was leaving Paul Reynolds's agency to start his own firm, and that he wanted her to come with him, she didn't hesitate to leave *Collier's*, sensing that while the position at Harold Ober Associates was secretarial, the opportunity to advance might exist, a hunch that was rewarded a few years into her employment.

She'd stumbled upon Mr. Ober's extracurricular activities by accident. Late one night at the office, after Mr. Ober had caught his train to Connecticut, and Max had gone for the day, she innocently intercepted a call from a distressed representative from the Morgan Library who wanted to hire Mr. Ober to track down a rare manuscript that had gone missing. Miss Doling had been quite confused at first, but the Morgan librarian was insistent about Mr. Ober's reputation in these matters, which she planned to laugh about with her boss in the morning. But when she mentioned the late-evening caller, Mr. Ober looked grim faced and accepted the message without comment, and certainly without mirth. From then on, Miss Doling noted oddities around the office that pointed to Max's being in the know, and possibly a willing participant. And also Wilson. Max seemed relieved when Miss Doling revealed what she knew, though it was Miss Doling who suggested that Mr. Ober's modesty about his hobby be preserved. If he didn't want talk about it around the office, so be it.

The workshop now ended, she disposed of the cup of coffee she'd been nursing, which had grown cold during the last twenty minutes of class, when she'd answered eager students' questions about whom agents were looking for. The answer that there *was* no answer was never satisfying, yet it inspired boundless hope.

The air had warmed, and Miss Doling tucked her satin scarf into her bag as she moved through the student body toward Julavits Hall. Professor O'Hara had tipped her off that the night classes were run by Columbia Community Education, a self-sustaining entity not affiliated with the university, though they had a basement office and access to classrooms after hours.

The eager, competent-looking woman with tightly curled red hair behind the desk in the windowless warren was startled by Miss Doling's appearance in the CCE office. The nameplate on her desk identified her as Robin Finn.

"Are you here to register for a class?" Miss Finn asked hopefully. She had a clear and incisive manner of speaking.

Miss Doling shook her head. "I'm trying to get some information on a student."

Miss Finn screwed up the tiny features on her freckled face. "Is there anything wrong?"

"It's a matter of some delicacy, I'm afraid. A Jane Doe has turned up in the city morgue, and we think she may have been a student in one of your secretarial classes."

Miss Finn turned pale. "Oh, how terrible."

Miss Doling nodded solemnly. "Yes, it is."

"We keep a binder of our students. If you can let me have her name."

"We believe her name is Miss Smith."

Miss Finn opened the thick black binder on the counter.

"A common name," she said casually, masking her distress.

"The course likely would've been last spring."

Miss Finn set the binder down.

"Oh, that's easy," she said. "I teach the spring class."

"Wonderful," Miss Doling said. She was cognizant of the doubtful look that clouded Miss Finn's face, a worry that she would be of no help, and Miss Doling knew it would be important to nourish her confidence in order to mine her memory for the relevant details.

"But I don't remember a Miss Smith."

"She might've gone by her married name, Mrs. Kelly."

"Irish?"

"Russian, actually."

Miss Finn searched her mind, desperate to help.

"Or perhaps she called herself Miss Salzman."

"My, so many names."

"You can see our difficulty."

"The class roster might jog my memory," Miss Finn said, flipping through the binder. She found the page and scanned it with a nicely manicured finger. "Oh yes, I remember this class now. A larger class than we normally enroll. The numbers go up and down, depending."

"I'm sure," Miss Doling said softly. "May I look at the register? I might recognize a name."

"Of course."

Miss Finn bit her lip while Miss Doling studied the class roster.

"Does anyone stand out in your mind from this class?"

"Most students in night classes are pretty tired by the end of the day. The classes are often unmemorable."

"I see there was a man enrolled in this class."

Miss Finn's face lit up. "Yes, I remember that now. A very nice man."

"Isn't it a bit unusual for a man to be taking a secretarial course?"

Miss Finn nodded in agreement. "It is unusual. He's the first that I know of."

"Do you remember anything about this Mr. Jeffries?"

"He was exceedingly polite. And was an alert student."

"Did he give any indication about why he was taking the class?"

Miss Finn thought for a moment, the red curls on her head vibrating.

"He was about to start a job at an import/export company and wanted to brush up on his office skills."

"Did he give the name of his employer, by chance?"

"Why, yes," Miss Finn answered. "I only remember it because the name is the same as my husband's: Martin Exports. Do you think that's useful?"

"It's hard to say," Miss Doling admitted.

Miss Finn exhaled loudly and a silence descended. Miss Doling wondered if she should copy down the roster in the event that it would be useful to Mr. Ober. Anything was better than returning empty-handed. There was every chance that the office clerk at Martin Exports wouldn't remember anything about anyone else in the night class. Or he may have moved on to another place of employment.

"I remember now," Miss Finn said brightly. "After a couple of classes, Mr. Jeffries would arrive and leave with a girl from class. I wondered if it was a burgeoning romance."

"Which girl?"

Miss Finn searched the list, her finger landing on the name Miss Clarke.

18

THE ASHEN FACE PEERING from the darkness inside Dilly's shook no in answer to Ober's question.

"He's not in. Best to make an appointment."

"Will you tell him it's Harold Ober?"

The door was closed without comment, but Ober waited as the late-lunch foot traffic whizzed by. Ober knew Carmine Russo wouldn't give him an appointment outside of normal business hours, but he preferred to put his questions to Russo without the carnival atmosphere of Dilly's when it was open. He was about to join the human tributary and walk back to his office when the door opened fully. The ashen face was connected to a lanky body clothed in a cheap suit the same ashen color as its skin.

"He's with someone, but you can wait."

The powerful smell of ammonia caused Ober's eyes to water, and it took a moment after the door was closed again for his eyes to adjust to the tableau, the velvet couches and gilded mirrors, now shrouded in darkness save for the far corner table, which was lit by white sunlight from a skylight Ober hadn't previously noticed. Carmine Russo was seated at the table, a glass of water in front of him. Across the table a thick, nervous man with a mustache, dressed in a white shirt and a faded candy-apple-colored tie, was slouched in his chair. Next to him was a frail old woman with cotton-white hair, wearing a loose-fitting floral-patterned pink dress that hung off her slight frame like a sail in a breeze.

Russo's doorman retook his position behind the nervous man and the old woman, looming over them, so that it looked like they were sitting under a thin gray tree.

Russo glanced at Ober but made no attempt to acknowledge his presence. Instead he turned to the nervous man and said, "I see what you're saying, but do you see what I'm trying to say?"

The nervous man studied his folded hands, which were in his lap. He nodded slowly. "It's just that we need the money now."

"But if you let it ride, you may win twice that amount, or more," Russo said earnestly.

The old woman gave a start. "You're trying to cheat us! We've been playing the numbers for most of our lives, and we've never won as much as a nickel. Well, now we've won and we want our money."

Russo took a sip of his water. "I wouldn't expect you to immediately understand what it is I'm proposing—"

"You're trying not to pay us!"

The nervous man put his hand on the old woman's arm. "Calm down, Momma. We can listen to what Mr. Russo has to say."

"Thank you, Mr. Conway. All I'm asking for is the opportunity to be heard."

Ober sensed the conversation was gaining momentum and took a seat on a nearby velvet divan. No one noticed, and he felt as if he'd sunken from view entirely.

"Momma's correct, though," Mr. Conway said. "We do need this money."

Russo took another drink of water and let his glass fall against the tabletop with a loud bang.

"I thought I was going to be heard on the subject."

"We'll listen, yes," Mr. Conway assured him in the manner of a child chastised by its parent.

"But you're saying regardless you want to be paid."

Mr. Conway gave a confused look.

"What I meant was that we aren't opposed to hearing what you have to say about—"

Russo glared at him, his nostrils pulsating in the white light. "So you want me to waste my breath on the likes of you two just so you can tell me, 'No thanks, give us our money'?"

Mr. Conway sat up in his chair alertly.

"We mean no offense, Mr. Russo. But this money is going to help us out a great deal."

"We shouldn't have to beg for our money!" the old woman squawked.

"Mrs. Conway, if you please," Russo said calmly.

Mr. Conway again tried to comfort his mother by touching her on the arm, but she shirked his hand.

"You are living up to your reputation, Mr. Russo," the old woman said, a little less forceful, as if she'd been made to accept a fact she violently disagreed with.

Russo smiled. "I hope my reputation isn't as bad as that. I asked my man to send Mr. Conway to me so that I could share the wisdom of my many years' experience."

The old woman harrumphed. "Some experience!"

Russo ignored her.

"Not only will you stand a chance to win more money tomorrow than you've won today, you'll also increase the percentage of winnings I personally pay to the policy broker in your neighborhood, who in turn uses the money to keep the peace on your street, and your neighbors' streets. It's really a matter of civic duty."

"The grocer pays protection money to keep our block safe," Mrs. Conway informed him. "But I suppose you already know that."

The ashen-faced goon standing over them swayed, and Mr. Conway flinched.

Russo raised his glass and slowly sipped the remaining water. He set the empty glass carefully on the table.

"It's apparent," he said slowly, reaching into the pocket of his herringbone suit, "that I'm wasting my time here." He produced a roll of money the size of a fist, and one of the Conways gasped. "So here's your money." He peeled off a number of bills and piled them in the middle of the table.

Mr. Conway nodded gratefully and carefully picked up the bills one at a time. He counted them twice and then gave a puzzled look.

"Anything wrong?" Russo asked innocently.

"With all pardons, but it's twenty short," Mr. Conway said.

Russo laughed. "Are you sure?"

"I counted it twice."

"Why don't you count it again, to be sure."

Russo smiled at his associate and the associate smiled back.

Mr. Conway counted the money a third time.

"What did you get?"

"Twenty short," Mr. Conway said in a timid voice.

"I've been misinformed," Russo said with a smile. "I was told Paddies couldn't count past their ten fingers."

Mr. Conway smiled as if he were in on the joke, but Mrs. Conway gripped her black purse and rocked in her chair.

Ober scuffed his shoes against the floor, hoping to draw attention away from the insult, but again he felt alone in the dark.

"That's our money!" Mrs. Conway hissed.

"But it's in my pocket," Russo said.

"A common dago thief!"

The smile passed from Russo's lips. "You're forgetting your manners, Mrs. Conway."

"You never had any," Mrs. Conway said.

Russo considered her for a moment and then reached again into his pocket. He let the roll of bills unfold completely, the money fanning out before them.

"You've got plenty. Give us ours," Mrs. Conway demanded.

"I'm going to give you your money, ma'am," Russo said. "Don't despair. Even though you've been uncivil and come into my establishment and insulted me—"

"You insulted us first!"

"—and interrupted me with your insolent bog tongue, I'm going to pay you."

Russo waded up a dollar bill and threw it at Mrs. Conway, who let out a sharp cry as the money glanced off her cheek.

Mr. Conway started and then made a move for the crumpled-up bill, but the ashen-faced man grabbed both his shoulders, keeping him in place.

Russo continued to wad up dollar bills and bounce them off Mrs. Conway, who flinched each time but otherwise sat stoically.

"I hope this money is as useful to you as you claim," Russo said.

The clumps of dollar bills collected around the feet of the Conways.

"You'll never see this kind of money again in your miserable lives, so enjoy it."

Russo looked at the pile of money in his hand.

"How much is that now?" he asked.

"You owe us two more dollars," Mrs. Conway said softly.

Russo studied Mrs. Conway's downcast face.

"I'll keep two for my troubles," he said. "You've kept Mr. Ober waiting far too long. He shouldn't have to wait on a couple of run-down micks."

Ober stood upon hearing his name. The Conways dropped to their knees and scavenged the money from the floor while Russo laughed. They gave Ober a sullen look as they were rushed out by Russo's associate, who opened the front door only wide enough to squeeze them out onto the pavement.

"Thank you for waiting," Russo said as he approached.

"I'm sorry to call on you without an appointment," Ober said.

The genial smile Russo meant to employ was spoiled by a grimace. "What kind of a man would put his own mother through something like that?"

Ober refrained from comment, still a little sickened by what he'd witnessed. He'd come to ask a couple of questions and was eager to ask them and be gone.

"And who comes into my place of business and calls me a dago?" Russo asked incredulously. "I'm not fresh off the boat. I'm a well-respected member of the business community. For God's sake, just the other night I sat at the very same table with Mayor Walker!"

Ober glanced at the table, hoping the matter would pass.

"You probably never have to deal with the sort of lower order I do," Russo said conspiratorially. "You believe those two?" A wild light shone in his dark eyes.

"I didn't really catch much of it," Ober demurred.

"Get me a drink, will ya?" Russo said to his associate, who was floating in the shadows around them. To Ober he said, "Now what can I do for you?"

Ober cleared his throat.

"You'll remember the other night I was here asking about the woman who had been murdered—"

"What's your interest?" Russo asked.

"She was the secretary of a friend of mine. They had traveled from Los Angeles to New York for a business trip—"

Russo laughed despite himself.

"But she used to live in New York," Ober said. "Which I think you know."

Russo eyed him. "What makes you think I know that?"

"Because she was your girlfriend."

Russo grinned. "Was she?"

Russo's associate handed him a scotch on the rocks with both hands.

"Go get my money back," he instructed, and the ashen face nodded. "And tell David Ryan I don't want any more Irish winners from that neighborhood." The associate nodded again and slithered out the front door.

Russo took a long drink and blanched. Nothing was satisfactory to him, it seemed.

"What were you saying?"

"That Miss . . . what did she call herself?"

"How can you come in here and make accusations when you don't even know her name?"

Ober flushed. "She appeared to have several. Her married name was Mrs. Kelly—"

"I don't know anything about her being married," Russo said defensively.

"Not to worry. The marriage was a mail-order one."

Russo's face lit up. "Layers upon layers, eh?"

"So it would seem."

"I knew her as Vera Miller."

"And she was your girlfriend."

"Okay, she was. What of it?"

Ober measured his next sentence out a beat at a time.

"She told you she was pregnant."

Russo waved off the suggestion. "She wasn't pregnant."

"I didn't say she was pregnant. She *told* you she was pregnant. And you gave her money to go to Los Angeles to have the child. But there was no child."

Russo drained the last of his scotch and dropped the empty glass onto a nearby couch, where it landed soundlessly.

"Yeah, yeah, yeah," he said. "What of it?"

"Did you know she'd come back to New York?"

Russo shook his head.

"Was she drinking here the night of her death?"

Russo cackled. "That little bitch was a lot of things, but not stupid. She wouldn't have come within a mile of here."

"Yet she ended up on your stoop."

"If you're suggesting I had anything to do with her death . . ."

Ober remained quiet, hoping Russo would finish the thought and begin another, but his voice trailed off and Ober could see he was in a high state of agitation.

"How did your waitress come to be wearing her necklace, then?"

"You writing a book about all of this?" Russo sneered.

Ober felt a tingling sensation run down his legs. "As I said, I'm only trying to help a friend."

"Tell your friend he shouldn't consort with such trash. That was my mistake."

"Who stripped the body?"

Russo shrugged. "How should I know? I wasn't even here that night."

Ober sensed Russo was not telling the truth, but he didn't need to hear him admit it. He extended his hand.

"I hope I haven't interrupted your day."

"This day is already shot to hell," Russo said. "But that's business."

Ober turned to let himself out.

"That mick Wilson still working for you?"

Ober flinched but remained silent.

"The day he went to work for you, he got an honest streak and quit coming around," Russo lamented. "If everyone in midtown becomes so respectable, how is a man like me to make a living?"

19

MAX WASN'T SURE WHY he'd asked to tag along with Lily to Yonkers. He'd passed along the address he'd found for Philip Slater to Jeannette Barnes, and had intimated but left vague the details of Slater's extracurricular sex life. She'd accepted the information with a nervous joke about how lucky she'd been not to have gone along with him to the party he'd been trying to drag her to, and had thanked Max for his time and energy. He'd turned down her offer of paying him for his time.

He'd even sent an anonymous tip to Sergeant Roosevelt, not just informing him of Edmonds's photography business, but also suggesting that Edmonds had information about what had happened on the roof of the Dixon estate. Max hadn't an inkling about whether or not that was true, but Edmonds's threat had resonated with him, and in the interest of self-preservation he'd put Roosevelt onto the druggist.

And yet when Lily told him she was taking the train to Yonkers for a trip to the historical society to research a night circus from the late 1800s for the novel she'd been writing since forever, he volunteered to keep her company. The train conductor with the strict part in his black, oily hair and a two-day-old beard punched their tickets as the train lurched forward. Ahead in the car, someone sneezed, and it sounded like a flushed toilet.

Lily pressed her knees against the seat in front of her and stared out the window at the passing cityscape.

"Have you mentioned my novel to your boss?" she asked casually.

Max shook his head no.

"I wouldn't want someone to steal your idea," he said. "And the walls have ears."

Lily swatted at his arm, as he'd hoped.

"I hope they have some good stuff about this night circus," she said. "It's a plot point."

"I thought your book was loosely based on the unsolved Taylor case out in Hollywood, the director who was murdered. You had that great title."

"*We're So Famous.*"

"Right. I thought that was a good idea for a novel."

"But that would have to be a detective novel. I want to be a serious writer."

"You originally said it was going to be a satire of sensational celebrity culture. That sounded serious."

Lily rolled her eyes. "Readers *like* celebrity culture. They don't want to be browbeaten about how facile they are for being fascinated with celebrities."

"Maybe you could write it in a way that they don't know they're being browbeaten," Max offered.

"Trust me, this night circus idea is better. More metaphor."

The train braked suddenly and Lily covered her ears.

"I hate that sound."

Max bought two coffees from the café cart when it came around, and they sat staring ahead, each occasionally watching out the window as the train headed north. Max realized he'd been denying the truth about why he'd asked to accompany Lily to Yonkers, that there was something inside him that made him thirst for justice. He didn't possess Mr. Ober's equanimity, a quality he admired about his boss, whose passions were never inflamed. Only the business about Schellinger, whose acquittal of murder had outraged almost

everyone, seemed to cause Mr. Ober anguish. The evidence had so
strongly indicated Schellinger as the murderer of his girlfriend that
it was improbable that it could be anyone else, as his defense had
suggested. The verdict had come early enough in the day to make the
afternoon papers, and Max had gone running into Mr. Ober's office
when he heard a loud slam. But he'd ducked behind his screen when
he saw that it was only his boss reacting to the news.

As the train glided along, Max dreamed up various scenarios
involving his confrontation with Jeannette Barnes's boyfriend. In all
of them, he was cast as the avenging hero. In some of them, physical
violence was called for and he imagined himself standing over Philip
Slater's vanquished body like a prizefighter, though Max had never
thrown a punch in his life.

"He's married," Lily said clairvoyantly.

"What?"

"Philip Slater. He's married. Has a kid. Is that what you're
coming to find out?"

"How do you—"

"Jeannette told me. She watched him from down the street after
you gave her the address."

"She said she wasn't going to do anything."

Lily shrugged. "I guess she had a change of heart. It's a woman's
prerogative."

"Was she upset?"

"It was hard to tell."

Max sipped his coffee, which tasted strongly of having been
burned. A man in a gray fedora sitting across from them had a
coughing spell as the train crossed into the Bronx.

"If you want to do some improv on the guy, I'm game," Lily said
mischievously.

The white-and-green clapboard house listed at the address
Max had given Jeannette Barnes sat on a quiet cul-de-sac. Max and
Lily had taken the number 2 trolley line to the end, landing among
the only shopping in the area. Max had noted his reflection in the

window of Ulrich's fountain shop and momentarily wished for a cold Coca-Cola for courage, but Lily had skipped ahead at a fast clip, eager to play her part.

The Slater home resembled the other houses on the dead-end street. Max raised a hard fist and knocked loudly. Lily gave a yip when his fist landed, barely able to contain her excitement.

Philip Slater opened the door tentatively, smiling as a question crept across his brow. He was lithe, with a shock of brown hair and a prominent forehead. His weak chin gave his face the appearance of melting into his neck. He generally matched the subject of the photo Jeannette Barnes had given him.

"Can I help you?"

"My name is Harding, and this is my associate. We've taken the train up from New York," Max said, parceling out the threat against Philip Slater incrementally.

Slater furrowed his brow. "Yes?"

"We're looking into a matter on behalf of Jeannette Barnes."

Slater flinched at the sound of Jeannette's name, and Max felt a surge within. He hadn't expected a confession, or even an admission, but the flinch was satisfying.

"I don't know anyone by that name."

"Oh?" Max asked, showing off for Lily a little. "You are Mr. Philip Slater?"

"I am."

"Of Williams College?"

Slater raised an eyebrow in alarm.

"Who is it?" a voice called from down the hallway. Mrs. Slater, a slender blonde with wire-framed glasses, appeared with an infant sleeping on her shoulder.

"It's nothing, dear," Slater said sternly. "This gentleman has a wrong man."

Having been satisfied by Slater's squirming, Max was about to give an insincere apology to Mrs. Slater for taking any of her time, when Lily chimed in, her voice dripping with doubt.

"You're not the Philip Slater, Williams College alum, who works in bonds and knows Miss Jeannette Barnes?" she asked, leaning in as she spoke.

"Philip didn't go to college," Mrs. Slater said flatly. "And he works at his brother's garage here in Yonkers."

Max could feel the Slaters aligning against them, but Lily continued in her harangue.

"Do you own a camera?" she asked pointedly.

With his wife squarely in his corner, Philip Slater felt emboldened. "Doesn't everyone?"

Max touched Lily's wrist, worried that she was going to bring the whole matter out into the light in front of Mrs. Slater in an attempt to embarrass the woman's husband.

"We're led to believe Philip Slater, Williams College alum, who works in bonds and who knows Miss Jeannette Barnes intimately, is something of a camera aficionado."

"We just have an old Metrolux. A wedding gift from Cynthia's mother."

Lily regarded Mr. Slater. Max felt the conversation could go one of two ways and suddenly worried that the Slaters might call the police. He said, "We'll be on our way, then, back to New York, to continue our investigation."

Philip Slater followed them down the walkway but stopped when Max and Lily passed through the open gate. Max glanced over his shoulder and saw Slater smile at him. Max's heart jumped into his throat and he felt his pulse in his eyes. Philip Slater wouldn't be punished, he knew, and Jeannette Barnes would just be another casualty of his selfishness. The thought preoccupied him on the way back to New York, his anger turning to sadness as the train crossed back into the city. He wished Lily had returned with him instead of taking the later train to facilitate her research. He longed for her comforting presence.

20

"IT IS YOU, ISN'T IT?" Ober asked. He held out the mail-order catalog, open to the page with the chambermaid's picture. He'd been flipping through the pages casually, the black-and-white photos taking on a sameness until the features of one jumped out at him.

The chambermaid at the Byrne Hotel glanced nervously at the manager.

"Answer him," the manager said sternly.

"Will I lose my job, sir?"

"That remains to be seen. But answering these gentlemen's questions is in your favor."

Roosevelt loomed in the background, summoned by Ober to meet him at the hotel. Together, the three men formed a circle around the tiny chambermaid in the quiet hallway. She'd been fearful when they approached her cart, and Ober was mindful of not frightening her into silence.

"It's not a very good picture of you," Ober said kindly. "It doesn't do you justice."

The chambermaid gave a half smile.

"But it *is* you, correct?"

The chambermaid nodded.

"Anna Krupin. From Ivanovo." Ober reached into his pocket and produced the compact engraved with the letters *AK*. "And so this is yours."

The chambermaid took the compact and clutched it in her hand, happy for its return.

"Thank you, sir," she said timidly.

The manager was called away to tend to a guest on another floor, and Ober was glad of his leave-taking.

"You can speak freely," Ober said. "You knew the missing woman?"

The chambermaid nodded timidly. Her large brown eyes were rimmed with tears, and she had a nervous habit of swaying.

"What name did you know her by?"

"Vera Rosovsky." The chambermaid's voice was faint and it died as it reached the listener's ear.

"Did you also know Marina Antipova?"

"No, sir."

"She goes by the name Mrs. Anderson here in America. She called on Miss Rosovsky here at the hotel two days after she checked in."

"Mrs.," the chambermaid corrected him.

"Pardon me?"

"Mrs. Rosovsky."

Ober tipped his chin toward the dim hall lighting.

"What is it?" Roosevelt asked.

"She was already married," Ober announced. "Back in Russia. Is that right?"

The chambermaid nodded again.

"The artist relayed that she was in fear for her life from her husband, who would scream at her in Russian, but when I visited Mr. Kelly at his luncheonette in the South Street Seaport, I determined that he doesn't speak Russian."

Roosevelt laughed.

"But that, in and of itself, didn't exonerate Mr. Kelly," Ober added. "I thought perhaps the secretary was putting on a piece of theater for Mr. Clarke, to impress upon him how dire her situation really was."

"But Mrs. Anderson clearly knew she was still married back home," Roosevelt said.

Ober nodded thoughtfully. "It might be the secret at the heart of her denial about knowing Mrs. Rosovsky. Though it could be something else, too."

Roosevelt asked the chambermaid:

"And in what capacity did you know Mrs. Rosovsky?"

"Mr. Rosovsky was my piano teacher back home. He gave lessons in their flat. He was heartbroken when she left him for America. She just disappeared. He was frantic. Said he would search the ends of the earth for her."

The chambermaid caught her breath but continued to sway as she held on to her cleaning cart.

"What tipped you off when you saw the reservation for Miss Salzman?" Ober asked.

"I wasn't sure, but I remembered that Vera Salzman was the name of their downstairs neighbor. She was always complaining about the piano. It's a very uncommon name, Vera. So I mailed her a registration card with a note that the hotel needed it before she arrived."

"And then you sent it to her husband in Russia, thinking he would recognize the handwriting. Or not."

The chambermaid burst into tears. "I only wanted him to have a chance to see her again!"

"So it was the husband who showed up here pretending to be her brother," Roosevelt said finally.

"No, sir," the chambermaid sniffled. "He never showed up."

"But you thought maybe he had," Ober countered. "When you discovered Miss Salzman's hotel room in disarray, you thought he'd come and they'd had a fight. Which is why you cleaned it up, putting everything back in its place. You were in such a hurry you didn't notice that you'd dropped your compact."

"I was just scared. Please don't tell on me, sir."

A woman dressed in a crepe shift dress, a fur stole over her shoulders, exited her room and was startled to see a police officer in the hallway.

"Is there any problem?" she asked as she whisked by.

"Nothing to worry about, ma'am," Roosevelt said. "Just routine."

The woman bounced away and exited through a door marked for the stairs.

"Did Mrs. Rosovsky recognize you?" Ober asked.

"Yes," the chambermaid admitted.

"What was her reaction?"

"At first she seemed happy. She asked how long I'd been over and things like that."

"Did she ask about her husband?" Roosevelt wanted to know.

The chambermaid shook her head no. "But she said not to say that I'd seen her. She was afraid of someone in New York knowing that she'd come back."

"Any idea who?" Roosevelt asked.

"She didn't say, sir."

Roosevelt glanced at Ober, who nodded solemnly.

"I'm sorry to be the bearer of such bad news," he said. "But Mrs. Rosovsky is dead."

The chambermaid gasped.

"She was found murdered. Someone beat her badly and left her for dead."

Ober reached for the chambermaid as she collapsed against her cart in tears. She let out a wail and he patted her on the back.

"It's all my fault!" she moaned.

"We don't know that," Ober said plainly.

The chambermaid's moans subsided and she composed herself, wiping away her tears with the backs of her small hands. She sniffled and searched her apron for a tissue.

"What happened to her luggage?" Ober asked suddenly. "When you cleaned the room. I assume it was still there."

The chambermaid told them that it was, and she led them to the coatroom where she'd stashed it under a fictitious name.

<u>21</u>

"A MISS DOLING AND HER ASSISTANT, SIR," Jeffries announced

"Do they have an appointment?"

"They do not," Jeffries said.

"What do they want?"

"They wouldn't say. Only that they must speak with you."

The rotund pink man in the pressed white shirt a size too big shrugged his massive shoulders.

"Interrupt us in five minutes."

Jeffries nodded.

"Also, tell Kaminsky about the change in venue for today."

Jeffries nodded again. It was a ruse they used on the rare occasions when they had visitors at Martin Exports.

A moment or two later, he returned with an elegantly dressed woman and a rough-hewn boy of not more than nineteen.

"Miss Doling, sir," Jeffries said, giving a slight bow. "And her associate."

Jeffries closed the door behind him as he exited.

"Thank you for seeing us on short notice," Miss Doling said.

Wilson stood a step or two behind Miss Doling. He was used to having his orders come from Mr. Ober and had been confused when Miss Doling asked him to accompany her to the Flatiron Building, between Fifth Avenue and Broadway. Miss Doling had always been cordial with him, but he felt inferior to her, and in moments of self-honesty, he was infatuated with her elegance. He always felt a jolt in his step when he smelled her discreet creamy-vanilla perfume in the office.

The fat man wedged behind his teak desk, itself wedged into the telescoping corner office, looked displeased. Over his shoulder and out the window Wilson glimpsed the Empire State Building. He'd visited the observatory at the top of the Empire State Building with his brothers on a dare for their Christmas money. His younger brothers knew he was afraid of heights and had hoped to relieve him of the silver half-dollar he'd been given at Christmas, but Wilson had worked up courage that cold December day and made the agreed-upon lap around the top of the tall, tall skyscraper, collecting his brothers' two half-dollar pieces as a reward. His strategy had been to slit his eyes, to shorten his field of vision. Still, he couldn't help but be amazed at the jungle of concrete buildings below, all adorned with Christmas snow. The Flatiron Building had stood in relief to the rest. On any given day, it looked like a slice of wedding cake. The unusually shaped building had been built on the triangular piece of property that bordered Madison Square Park, and there were stories that the wind effect created by the drafts coming through the open park and sluicing down either side of the Flatiron was powerful enough to raise women's dresses to their knees. From the top of the Empire State Building that day, the Flatiron building, covered in snow, had appeared to have an extra-thick layer of frosting. Standing inside Martin Exports now, Wilson was amazed at how the walls of the office narrowed to a windowed point, an obvious architectural necessity, though one he hadn't considered the many times he'd stood on the sidewalk looking up, marveling at the ornate building.

"We're making inquiries about a Miss Clarke," Miss Doling said politely.

The exporter raised a quizzical eyebrow.

"What is your interest in Miss Clarke?" he asked thickly.

"We were led to believe that she was employed by you," Miss

Doling answered, dodging the exporter's question.

"Who told you that?"

The large wooden chair squeaked under the exporter's weight as he swiveled around and randomly chose some papers from the pink and yellow and white invoices stacked like a mountain range across the teardrop-shaped desk.

"Do you mean we have bad information?" Miss Doling asked innocently.

"You're very adept at not answering my questions."

Miss Doling smiled but offered no rejoinder.

"Miss Clarke worked here for a few months," the exporter admitted casually. "What of it?"

"What was her role at Martin Exports?"

The exporter squinted. "Is she in any kind of trouble?"

"Now it's you who isn't answering my questions," Miss Doling said, smiling.

The exporter regarded Miss Doling, his manner darkening.

"She filled in for Jeffries on his day off," he said unconvincingly. "Light office duties."

On cue, Jeffries appeared with the message that the exporter had an important phone call.

"I'm sorry not to have been of any help," the exporter said, meaning exactly the opposite.

"Thank you for your time," Miss Doling said sweetly.

Jeffries ushered them out, closing the door. Wilson listened for the exporter to pick up the receiver on his desk and pretend to have a conversation, but the ruse didn't extend that far.

Jeffries reminded Wilson of all those strivers who took the bus from his neighborhood in the Bronx into the city. He was a tall, sensible-looking man with an efficient manner. He was desperate to improve his circumstances, unable to see the tells that he'd come from a long line of immigrants who knew only hard work and labor and very little else. The sandalwood scent of his carefully pomaded hair, along with the closely cropped sides, irked Wilson. So, too, did the gold signet ring imprinted with a fire-breathing dragon Jeffries wore on his middle finger.

"You were asking about Miss Clarke?" Jeffries asked in a low voice.

"I believe you knew her, from Columbia?"

Wilson was amazed at how Miss Doling could deliver an accusation so that it sounded like banter.

Jeffries turned his head toward his boss's door, listening. Satisfied, he said:

"Yes, that's true. I met her at Columbia. How did you know?"

"We've had an interest in Miss Clarke for some time."

Jeffries twisted the ring on his finger, a nervous habit. "Do you have an idea where she's gone?"

The question surprised Miss Doling. "Did she quit without notice?"

Jeffries glanced again at his boss's door and nodded.

Impatience gripped Wilson. He knew he could knock Jeffries down on his knees and elbows and extract what Miss Doling wanted to know in a matter of minutes, but he would be embarrassed to employ such tactics in the presence of a fine lady like Miss Doling, and so he remained in the background.

"One day she just vanished," Jeffries said.

"What were her responsibilities here?"

"Errands, mostly. She helped me with some filing and typing, but mostly she made deliveries."

"What did she deliver?"

Jeffries was silent for a moment. He frowned as he debated something with himself.

"Information," he said.

"A go-between?" Miss Doling guessed.

"She could speak Russian," Jeffries explained. "Which was of great value to my boss."

"So you recruited her."

Jeffries nodded like a boy who had been caught stealing.

"What were the circumstances surrounding her disappearance?"

"She just quit coming in. I called the number we had for her, but it was a Chinese restaurant in Hell's Kitchen and they said she was gone. Has something happened to her?"

"I'm afraid so. She's been murdered."

Jeffries leaned against his metal desk, staggered by the information. "How?"

"Someone beat her to death in midtown."

Jeffries gasped. Wilson guessed he'd spent a considerable amount of energy avoiding the everyday violence of New York by sealing himself inside the Flatiron office and that he'd have had the same reaction to a mugging or a shotgun murder.

"Were any of her . . . assignments . . . dangerous?" Miss Doling asked.

Jeffries shook his head. "Nothing like that. She would deliver a package anonymously. Sometimes pick up a package left for us at a drop point."

"So she never had contact with anyone who might know her as an agent of this office?"

"She was to use the name Ginny if anyone asked. But no one ever did, to my knowledge. She took precautions not to be memorable. Dressed down, like she'd been instructed. She was very good for us."

Jeffries swallowed the tremor in his voice

"What was her last assignment before she disappeared?"

Jeffries laughed, and then frowned at his inappropriate response.

"Why is it funny?" Wilson wanted to know. He scowled at Jeffries. Perhaps the moment he'd hoped for had arrived.

"No, it's just . . . she was to inspect some clothing down in the garment district that we were exporting to Brazil. She volunteered, and she was an excellent dresser, so my boss agreed to let her go." He paused and then added, "We do have to keep up appearances."

"Did she ever talk about any of the people in her life?" Miss Doling asked.

"She lived with a roommate in Hell's Kitchen, but other than that, no."

"Yet she was fluent in Russian."

Jeffries smiled. "I didn't ask why. The less we knew about each other's personal lives, the better."

"I suppose that's true," Miss Doling agreed. "Thank you for your time."

"I hope some of it is of use."

Wilson opened the door for Miss Doling, but she stood in the transom and turned to Jeffries.

"Which agency?" she asked.

Jeffries paused as he walked toward his boss's door.

"I'd prefer not to say," Jeffries demurred.

Wilson waited for a cue from Miss Doling, but she nodded at Jeffries and they took their leave.

"Do you want the answer to your last question?" he asked as they exited the building.

"The answer hardly matters," Miss Doling said. She exchanged her glasses for her prescription sunglasses. Wilson thought the dark glasses made her look like a movie star. "Though it might be useful to know a little bit more about our man Jeffries."

Wilson understood. The arcade entrance at the front of the Flatiron Building, one side leading to Fifth Avenue and the other to Broadway, would be hard to cover. But he'd handled more-difficult assignments in the past, and he assured Miss Doling that he was up to the task.

Miss Doling pulled her fur-lined collar up around her neck against the cool wind barreling in from the park as she crossed Twenty-Third Street. She recognized the broad-shouldered figure waiting for her at the entrance of the park as that of Arnold Sutton, an amateur private detective who had once tried to convince her to help him find a writer for his memoir, which was little more than the story of a man in the right place at the right time: Sutton had been shopping for an overdue anniversary present for his wife when he'd spotted a notorious bank robber casually browsing in the next aisle. Sutton then tailed the bandit to his apartment in Little Italy and alerted the authorities, who swooped in. Sutton pocketed the healthy reward the government had been offering and used some of it to open his own private detective business. He had, as far as Miss Doling knew, failed to acquire any significant cases outside the odd cheating husband or missing piece of jewelry. She knew, too, that Sutton bore a grudge against Carmine Russo, who had tried to extort a portion of the reward money based on the fact that the bank robber had been apprehended in a building Russo owned. Sutton had refused to pay it, but there was a rumor that Russo had extracted the expected payment by force.

"Hallo," Sutton hailed her as she passed. He was a highly colored man with haggard charm. Whatever his deficiencies were as a detective, at least he looked the part with his fedora and plaid overcoat. His shoes, however, were recently shined and hardly worn, a sure sign of idleness.

"Mr. Sutton."

"Paying a visit to Martin Exports?"

"I'm sure I don't know what you mean," Miss Doling said with mock innocence.

"Save it," Sutton said. "I know about the Jane Doe."

Miss Doling knew from his memoir pitch that Sutton's cousin worked at Police Plaza.

"And?"

"And that she was found on Carmine Russo's doorstep. And I know how she was found."

Sutton indicated with an exaggerated look that he was to be taken seriously on the subject.

"How can I help you, Mr. Sutton?"

"Tell me what the exporter said."

"Which exporter?"

"I know about the secretarial course at Columbia. And that her classmate got her the job with the exporter."

"It sounds like you've been building quite a case," Miss Doling teased him.

"That rat Carmine Russo is at the bottom of whatever this is," Sutton said with a measure of bitterness.

"How are they connected, the exporter and Russo?" Miss Doling asked, testing how much Sutton actually knew.

Sutton grimaced.

"I'm working on it," he promised.

22

THE COMMOTION INSIDE Scribner Book Store was easy to spot. A crowd had gathered around Fitzgerald, who was borne aloft by a wooden footstool, in the fiction section. Fitzgerald read loudly from his new novel, which had garnered decent reviews, but which had failed to sell in the number of copies his two previous novels had. Ober had encouraged him to take the long view of the situation, but he sensed in Fitzgerald a panic about his celebrated status as an oracle for his generation, which occasionally led to episodes like the one playing out for Scribner's confused patrons.

Ober stood at the edge of the crowd. Fitzgerald teetered as he read, and Ober recognized the glassy look in his eyes. He waved when Fitzgerald glanced up, a signal Fitzgerald recognized, and to Ober's amazement, he stepped down and began apologizing profusely to the crowd, which dispersed and continued to browse the shelves.

Ober managed to extract the name of Fitzgerald's hotel and folded him into a cab with instructions for the cabdriver not to make any detours along the way. The afternoon air was pleasant, and Ober considered a quick walk around the pond in Central Park, as he sometimes did if he had a free moment, but his bookkeeper had discovered a number of discrepancies, and the rest of the day would be ruined by his having to pour over royalty statements for all his authors for the last two reporting periods. He prided himself on exacting every penny owed to his clients, but there was an associated cost, including the strain on his eyes.

The royalty statements would have to wait, he realized, when he recognized the figure of Mr. Kelly haunting the art-deco lobby of his office building. They exchanged pleasantries in the elevator, but the weary countenance worn by Mr. Kelly was a sure sign that he wasn't making a social call.

Max brought them both coffee as Mr. Kelly tried and failed to get comfortable in the chair across from Ober's desk. Kelly took a large gulp of the coffee and followed it with another.

"What brings you here today?" Ober asked.

"I'm being followed," Mr. Kelly said.

"Yes? Who is following you?"

"The government."

"Immigration?"

Kelly started.

"Did they contact you?" he asked, alarmed.

Ober shook his head. "No."

"Then how—"

"You married Vera Rosovsky for the purposes of obtaining her a green card, correct?"

Kelly lowered his head and then ran his fingers through his sandy-colored hair.

"I've never given a true answer to that question."

"I suppose you can't."

"The whole thing was my brother's wife's idea. She said her friend was desperate to get out of Russia, and my brother convinced me everything would work out."

Ober eyed him. "Did she say why Mrs. Rosovsky wanted so badly to leave her hometown?"

Kelly gave a cautious look. "She needed to get away from her husband."

"Those were her words?"

Kelly shook his head no. "Marina's."

"How was it arranged?"

"My brother paid the fee to the international travel agency and all the travel costs. He has a good job."

Ober stared out the window, thinking. "Is that all?"

Kelly rearranged himself in his chair but couldn't find a way to get comfortable.

"Vera gave me some money. About three hundred dollars. I used it to buy Decker's."

"We found close to that amount in a false compartment in her suitcase," Ober said.

"Maybe she was going to buy another husband," Kelly cracked. His words were an obvious attempt at masking his self-loathing.

"Did you ever question where a young girl in Russia would get that amount of money?"

"She said she'd been saving it up, from doing odd jobs."

"Did you believe that?"

Kelly drank the last gulp of his coffee.

"If you knew Vera, you would understand. She could be very sweet and very convincing."

"So you didn't suspect that she'd stolen the money from her husband?"

Kelly winced. "I wouldn't want to think that about her."

"Nevertheless."

"Nevertheless," Kelly said quietly.

"She swindled the same amount from Carmine Russo. Her disappearance must've caused you a headache."

Kelly bit his lip and said bitterly:

"We spent all that time trying to fool immigration and then she pulls a stunt like that. I even left her a note at Dilly's, begging her to return, but I never heard from her again."

"Where did you think she'd gone?"

Kelly shrugged. "I assumed Russo fixed her up."

"Is that when immigration got wise?"

"I made it worse by telling them that she'd gone back to Russia, thinking they'd let the matter drop. But they said she hadn't used her passport for travel. They track the Russian ones now, or so they say. From then on, they've paid me weekly visits, eating at Decker's, following me home, staking out my apartment. I never know if the person sitting next to me on the bus is an agent or not. I thought *you* were one of them."

"Did you never have feelings for your wife?" Ober asked tactfully.

"Do ... do you mean ... ," Kelly stammered, his face glowing red.

The color rose in Ober's face as well. "No, I mean when you were first living together. Those first days."

Kelly gave a look of relief.

"We were more like roommates," he said. "We palled around with my brother and his wife a lot. Movies, dinners, a show now and then. But it was strictly platonic with Vera."

Ober pondered:

"What about Mrs. Anderson? Is her marriage a happy one?"

"Oh yes! She and my brother are very much in love."

"What circumstances did Mrs. Anderson leave behind in Russia?"

"She was always telling stories about her poor relations. No education, no jobs beyond piecemeal work. Stuff like that."

Ober nodded appreciatively.

"I have a friend who tells me stories about the hard times in Russia," he said. "I assume Mrs. Anderson's family is too poor to visit her in New York."

Kelly answered in the affirmative, again stressing their extreme poverty.

"Have the Andersons found themselves a suitable replacement in their social life?" Ober asked.

"They don't go out as much as they used to. Certainly not as much as Mrs. Anderson would like."

The phone buzzed on Max's desk and he answered it. Miss Doling asked to see him, and while he was reluctant to leave his boss and Mr. Kelly, the conspiratorial nature of her voice indicated that she'd chosen this exact moment for a conference, knowing Mr. Ober would be otherwise occupied.

"Excuse me," Max said.

His boss nodded that it was okay for him to step out.

Wilson was already in Miss Doling's office, leaning in the corner. Miss Doling recounted what she had uncovered at Columbia, as well as her visit to Martin Exports.

"Arnold Sutton has been sniffing around this too," Miss Doling said.

"He anywhere close?" Max asked. He knew his boss tolerated Sutton but preferred Sutton to keep his distance. Max knew part of his job at the office was to keep people like Sutton from claiming too much of Mr. Ober's time.

"He's blinded by the connection to Carmine Russo," Miss Doling answered. "He's only interested in pinning the whole thing on him."

"Regardless of whether or not it's the truth of the matter," Max said.

Miss Doling smiled. The boss's protégé had absorbed his righteous streak.

"Wilson followed Jeffries after he left work," she said.

"Anything?" Max asked hastily. He was counting the minutes he'd been absent his post and worried that Ober would come looking for him.

"I'll let him tell you," Miss Doling said, teasing.

Wilson smirked. "He went to Molly Adler's."

Wilson waited for a reaction, but Max was unsure who Molly Adler was.

"I told you," Wilson said to Miss Doling.

"Is it a speakeasy?" Max asked. "Owned by Russo?"

Wilson let out a cackle.

"No, dear," Miss Doling answered. "It's a house of ill repute."

Max felt the tips of his ears flame. He was caught between Wilson's knowing smile and Miss Doling's sympathetic glance. It was Miss Doling who rescued him.

"I typed everything up, as usual," she said, handing him a plain envelope addressed to the post office box Ober kept for anonymous tips, the system they used when Miss Doling wanted to pass along information.

Max thanked her and returned to his desk.

"When you said you'd left a note for your wife at Dilly's, did you mean you mailed it or delivered it yourself?" Ober asked.

Kelly was so worn down that he was practically oozing out of his chair.

"I mailed it."

"You've never been there?"

"Never."

"So if someone said they saw you there, they'd be lying."

Kelly sat upright and straightened his legs. "Did someone say they saw me?"

"Not as of yet."

Kelly stood abruptly.

"Thank you for the coffee," he said.

Ober rose as well. "My pleasure."

Kelly reached out and Ober shook his hand. "May I rely on your discretion about my confessions?"

"You may."

Max showed Mr. Kelly to the door, and as he reentered the office, he unsheathed the note Miss Doling had typed up so that Mr. Ober couldn't see that the envelope had no postmark.

"Another anonymous tip, sir."

23

THE WIDE SEA OF PARQUET FLOORING created a dizzying effect for any who entered the lobby of the newly constructed high-rise apartments on West Seventy-Fifth Street. Harold Ober remembered the fanfare surrounding the building's grand opening a couple of years before. The press had been enamored of the architect's penchant for hidden stairways and trick doors, which lent the otherwise ordinary apartment building the air of having a secret identity. It was this mystique that had prompted Molly Adler to establish her clubhouse on the second floor, an emporium tastefully decorated with Oriental rugs, original paintings (some gifted from the artists), and Chippendale furniture kept for the purpose of lively conversation and interaction with the bevy of young, beautiful women who lived in apartments scattered through the building, their rent paid for by Adler. That the apartment building on West Seventy-Fifth Street was a bordello was an open secret, owing to Adler's shrewd business acumen, which included substantial payoffs to the police officers who frequented the clubhouse and the rooms upstairs. There were rumors that Mayor Walker was a frequent patron, and Ober had heard that the entire enterprise was underwritten by Carmine Russo.

Against the far wall of the cavernous lobby, a marble staircase with a gilded handrail took visitors and residents alike to a mezzanine, where a bank of elevators awaited. A lacquered wooden podium was nestled up against the stairwell, and a small man in a black-and-white suit sprung to life when Ober approached. It was still the dinner hour, and the concierge seemed surprised to have a guest at such an early hour.

Ober announced himself and his desire to visit the clubhouse above. The fresh-faced concierge copied Ober's name into a ledger kept in a secret drawer in the podium with a briskness that masked the young man's giddiness at his position. Ober guessed the boy was in a position to witness all kinds of behavior.

The clubhouse lived up to its reputation, and Ober sank into one of the oversized couches. The room was lit only by the setting sun peeking in through the shuttered windows, giving the clubhouse the appearance of a museum after dark, after all the patrons had gone for the day. The air was heavy with the smell of incense and stale cigarette smoke. Ober scanned the nearby antique bookshelf and noted the number of inscribed copies from contemporary writers, including a few of his own clients.

"Mr. Ober," a soft voice purred from behind him. He hadn't heard Molly Adler enter the room and guessed that she'd used one of her famous secret entranceways.

"Miss Adler, it's a pleasure."

Molly Adler was a short, obese woman with thick glasses and was clothed head to toe in a white satin chiffon dress. As she moved across the room, Ober was reminded of a cloud drifting in the sky.

"The pleasure is all mine," Miss Adler said as she sat opposite him, an antique mahogany leather-top coffee table between them. Her voice was full of coquetry. "Your name has floated around this room on numerous occasions."

Ober blushed. While he enjoyed his Yankee reputation, he knew it had been exaggerated among those who knew him, including his writers, who often compared their own vice-ridden lives against his for negative effect. But he made no moral judgments about the habits of others.

"In fact," Miss Adler continued as she retrieved a cigarette from a silver case engraved with two cherubs kissing, "Miss Hycner is upstairs. I believe she's one of yours." She offered the case to Ober, but he politely declined.

"Former client," he informed her.

"She *is* a handful." Miss Adler laughed kindly.

"Her choice, not mine," Ober clarified. Miss Hycner was an acid-mouthed magazine columnist whose take on modernity Ober enjoyed. He'd represented her in the early years of her career, but she'd abruptly ended their business relationship some time ago. There had been whispers of a crack-up, though Ober chose to believe the move had been part and parcel of Miss Hycner's independent spirit.

An awkward silence passed, which Ober broke by saying:

"This is a cozy room. The art is magnificent. All originals?"

"Gifts," Miss Alder replied.

Ober admired a naturalistic painting of a woman in repose he hadn't previously noticed.

"I like that one," he said approvingly.

"Did you really come here to talk about art?" Miss Adler asked archly.

"No, I came to ask about one of your clients."

Miss Adler tsked. "A girl never tells."

"I appreciate the confidential nature of your clientele," Ober said. "We have that in common."

"Yes, I suppose we do."

"And you must know that I wouldn't be here if it weren't a serious matter."

Cigarette smoke drifted above Miss Adler's mass of curly brown hair.

"I'm well protected, if that's what you mean."

"Nothing to do with that," Ober assured her. "I'm investigating the murder of a woman killed a couple of weeks ago."

Miss Adler grimaced. "I hate murders, of any kind."

Ober gave an appreciative smile. "I'm here about someone who knew the deceased. If you'll allow me to say his name, you can decide whether or not you have anything to contribute on the subject. Would that be satisfactory?"

Miss Adler exhaled a storm of smoke and nodded.

"The man's name is Jeffries."

Miss Adler's face betrayed no emotion. The thick lenses of her glasses made it impossible for Ober to read any kind of reaction. She sat before him like the stone Buddhas for sale to tourists in Chinatown. Then she shifted, her dress rustling as she repositioned her legs under her.

"A nasty piece of work," she said finally.

"You've had problems with him?"

"Banned him," she said matter-of-factly.

"On what account?"

"He's a rough customer. And not all of the girls go in for that sort of behavior."

"I'm under the impression that he visited recently."

Miss Adler gave a weak wave.

"He charms his way back in," she said. "But inevitably I have to tell him to go away for a spell."

"Know anything of his background?"

Miss Adler laughed.

"So nothing about where he's from, what he does for a living, none of that?"

"My dear," Miss Adler purred, "he could be a tugboat captain or heir to a fortune or disgraced royalty, for all I know."

"I appreciate that," Ober said.

Miss Adler snuffed out the remains of her cigarette in a tin ashtray shaped like a seashell. The leather top of the coffee table was pocked, and there was a tear in one corner.

"You're in need of some repairs, looks like."

"Generally," Miss Adler deadpanned.

"Jeffries ever have any problems with any of your other patrons?"

"He's a skulker, you know? Never really participates in any of the salon talk. I'm rather under the impression that he's a dimwit."

"What makes you say that?"

"He had no idea what the *New Yorker* was."

"You mean he doesn't read it?"

"No. I mean he didn't even know it was a magazine *to* read."

"We can deduce from that that he is not royalty," Ober laughed.

"Oh, you'd be surprised," Miss Adler countered.

"I'm sure. Does Jeffries drink?"

Miss Adler nodded.

"Excessively?"

"I wish. Drunks I can handle with ease."

"He only turns violent in chambers, then?"

"My girls have buzzers for when there are problems. And with him there's always a problem."

"Does he harm the girls?"

Miss Adler considered the question. "He once gave one of my girls a black eye. But mostly he left behind a trail of red skin and bruises."

"Does he resist when you eject him?"

"Yes, but my man is very persuasive."

"Jeffries ever get into a fight with him?"

Miss Adler laughed. "He's still alive, isn't he?"

Ober surveyed the room again. He pointed at the bookcase.

"I see you're the proud owner of the complete works of Arnold Sutton, private eye."

"I'm assured it's a one-of-a-kind edition," she laughed. "He printed it up for me. He likes everyone to know that he's a private detective. First one to hightail it when the police are in residence, though. But he's a harmless amusement."

Ober stood. "Will you give my regards to Miss Hycner? Ask her to drop in on me sometime."

"I shall." Miss Adler stayed seated and lit another cigarette. "And will you tell Mr. Fitzgerald that if his friend is missing a monogrammed dress shirt, I may know where it is."

24

"I DON'T APPRECIATE this intrusion on my time," Ober said sharply.

Norton settled the pretty, young girl with discreet makeup, wearing her Sunday best, in one of the chairs across from Ober's desk and then took the other.

"I thought we left it that I would bring Miss Deery around," Norton said innocently.

"You know well that is not the case." He nodded at the girl. He guessed she was in her late teens. "Miss."

"Charmed," Miss Deery said and smiled.

"Excellent manners, this one," Norton said admiringly.

"I can only give you a few minutes," Ober remarked.

Max took his cue and retreated behind the screen. He marked the time on the brass desk clock given Ober by an editor at Random House. He'd wait ten minutes and then interrupt.

"So as I was saying the other day ..." Norton's ability to resume previously suspended conversations had some claiming that he was a savant. Ober found the habit simply annoying. "Miss Rebecca Deery has an extraordinary angle on this affair."

Norton set the scene for Miss Deery by recounting the facts of the Schellinger case:

Schellinger's girlfriend, Alma Weeks, left her boardinghouse on Greenwich Street, having confessed to her cousin that she and Schellinger were to be married in secret that very night. Her cousin was worried about this revelation, as she'd witnessed Schellinger's affections toward a second boarder while he was awaiting Alma's return from running errands. The cousin tried unsuccessfully to persuade Alma against the marriage, never letting on that she knew anything against Schellinger. When Schellinger appeared at eight o'clock on the evening in question, the three sat in the drawing room with a couple of other boarders, exchanging pleasantries. The party quickly broke up, and Alma and Schellinger bid everyone good night.

"It was the last any saw of Alma Weeks alive," Norton said dramatically.

Ober knew all of this, and the rest, too. Though Norton didn't know it, Ober had gone every day of the trial. He'd often found himself glaring at Schellinger from the gallery as he listened to all the evidence:

The prosecution contended that Schellinger and Alma were met on Greenwich Street by a second man. The three were seen shortly after, riding together in a new yellow Austin 7 box saloon, a car owned by Schellinger and garaged at his home. Among the prosecution's witnesses was Aaron Quartullo, who was riding the late bus home from his dishwashing job through the dimly lit streets. Quartullo claimed the bus was overtaken by the distinctive car somewhere near eight thirty but that it held only the two gentlemen.

Also called to the stand was William Butcher, the closest neighbor to the clearing where Alma was found, and who discovered tire tracks driven curiously close to where the body lay in the fresh snow.

Lorraine Van Atta lived near the clearing too and testified that between eight and eight thirty she heard a scream pierce the winter night.

The defense moved to free Arthur Schellinger by placing blame on the deceased, painting Alma Weeks as a young woman who "sometimes appeared melancholy" and who would lie about her whereabouts when questioned about being out all night. It was the defense's contention that Alma had become pregnant by an unnamed suitor, such was the ever-deteriorating condition of her character, and not by Mr. Schellinger, as the prosecution contended. The defense called neighbors, friends, and business acquaintances to testify that the distinctive car seen by the cousin and later by Aaron Quartullo had remained in the garage the entire night. Expert after expert was called to dispute the prosecution's timeline about how long it would have taken to drive from the boardinghouse to the clearing and back to Schellinger's mansion on Millionaire's Row.

"Yes," Ober said impatiently.

Max checked his desk clock. The three minutes remaining stretched out like an hour as he eavesdropped on the recitation of facts everyone knew from the myriad newspaper accounts of the trial.

"You remember the dentist, Dr. Kern?" Norton asked.

Max knew his boss disdained being baited, conversationally or in any other way, and wasn't surprised by the silence that followed Norton's question. The newspapers had seized upon Dr. Kern, who was a surprise prosecution witness. Dr. Kern testified that he'd overheard Mr. Schellinger tell his office girl that he was soon to be an eligible bachelor again. The defense objected to this hearsay, but the reporters watching the trial stampeded one another in an effort to broadcast Dr. Kern's damaging testimony. As could have been expected, the defense dug deep into Dr. Kern's background, and when it was revealed that the dentist had lost his license the previous year and been censured in years previous to that for overly medicating his patients, he was quickly discredited as an eyewitness. And when he committed suicide a few days later by raising a pistol to his temple while sitting in the dentist's chair in his office, the book on Dr. Dustan closed with a thud.

"Miss Deery here is the office girl in question," Norton announced proudly.

Miss Deery glowed at the mention of her name.

The room quieted, but Miss Deery remained silent.

Ober cleared his throat. Max took this as his cue to interrupt, but as he stood from his desk, he heard his boss ask:

"How long were you employed by Dr. Dustan?"

Miss Deery flipped her long yellow hair over her shoulder. Ober had noticed the tick and it annoyed him greatly.

"A little over a year," she answered. Her tone was both haughty and eager.

"And I assume that you're here to confirm what Dr. Dustan claims to have overheard?"

"Go ahead," Norton interjected.

"It's true," Miss Deery said with a touch of zeal. "Poor Dr. Dustan. They should've believed him."

"What exactly did Mr. Schellinger say to you that day?" Ober asked.

"He asked me how old I was. And where I lived."

"Did you tell him?"

Miss Deery gave a shy smile.

"I don't tell strange men things like that." She paused, as if waiting for others to agree, and then said, "But he found out anyway."

"How did he find out?"

Miss Deery shrugged nonchalantly.

"He sent her a dozen roses," Norton said.

Miss Deery affected a bored look, as if this were a common occurrence.

"What else did he say?" Ober wanted to know.

"He said he was just getting out of a relationship and was feeling lonely," Miss Deery said. "He said he hoped to meet someone exciting and new."

"Anything else?" Ober asked.

Max could hear the doubt in Ober's voice.

"I spent the night at his house," Miss Deery added, "but I won't say anything about that now. I'll tell it in the book."

Norton sat back in his chair in mock astonishment. "Sensational, am I right?"

Ober rearranged some papers on his desk.

"I need to freshen up," Miss Deery said suddenly.

"It's in the hallway, left of the elevator," Norton told her.

Max stood and opened the office door for Miss Deery, who seemed surprised to see him.

"Well?" Norton asked.

"Where did you find her?"

"She came to me."

"You sure about that?"

"What do you mean?"

Ober leaned forward in his chair, and Max thought he saw a sneer creep across his boss's face and then disappear.

"She's lying."

"She's telling the truth," Norton insisted.

Ober shook his head. "Believe that if you want."

"You can't prove she's lying."

"If she publishes that story, Arthur Schellinger will sue her for libel and win," Ober said. "It will take successive generations of Deerys to pay the damages."

"But—"

Ober cut him off:

"She read about the dentist in the paper. But she never worked for him. Dr. Dustan's suicide conveniently allows her to claim otherwise, but as one who was actually in the courtroom, I can testify that Dr. Dustan was a fraudster, as the papers reported. He was a sad man with a failing practice who hoped to rejuvenate his business by having his name in the papers, the same papers that were eager to print the details of his corruption, but not the exchange between the prosecutor and the defense attorney I overheard during a break in the proceedings wherein the defense attorney took a measure of satisfaction in telling a detail he'd held back and had hoped to surprise Dr. Dustan with: that Mr. Schellinger wears dentures."

Ober let that fact sink in.

Norton grabbed his knees as if the wind had been knocked out of him.

"He'd still need a dentist," Norton said feebly, "to make adjustments."

"He does have a dentist," Ober said. "Who visits him at his home. If you know anything of the case, you know that Mr. Schellinger is a vain man. He prefers everyone to believe his teeth are his own."

Norton attempted a denial and Max interrupted with a reminder about Mr. Ober's lunch appointment.

"I'm sorry it's come to this," Ober said as he bade Norton good-bye. "But I must insist that you refrain from visiting me about this matter again. I'd rather not be so associated."

Norton's otherwise jovial manner paled, and Max could hear him berating Miss Deery in the hallway as they awaited the elevator.

"Will you ask Wilson in?" Ober said.

Max hustled down the hall to the messenger's desk, where Wilson sat asleep, his head resting on his crossed arms.

25

Wilson knew the number of different ways Mr. Ober could summon a person to his office, and he knew that when his boss sent him to deliver the message face-to-face, it meant he was to convince the person to acquit himself of whatever was occupying him at the moment to answer the request for his presence. Wilson knew he'd have an easy time with the exporter. He hadn't liked the man—he reminded him of the fishmonger in his neighborhood who cheated his customers by pressing his thumb on the scale—and he realized as he rode the elevator that he was looking forward to convincing the exporter of Mr. Ober's insistence. Part of him hoped that the exporter would resist.

Being inside the Flatiron Building now was as wondrous to Wilson as it had been the time before. His errands for Mr. Ober sometimes brought him to places he otherwise wouldn't be admitted to. Not like the strongman stuff he performed for Carmine Russo. He'd tricked himself into thinking the job with Russo was his only option, and then that it was temporary, grateful when Lily mentioned the open position she'd heard about at one of the Dominoes after parties.

The hall was empty as Wilson exited the elevator, save for a tall, friendly man with a close-cropped beard and a bowler hat. Insurance salesman, Wilson guessed.

"Is it raining?" the man asked.

"No," Wilson answered.

"The newspaper said it was going to rain today."

"What do the newspapers know?"

"That's true." The man laughed heartily. "Very wise indeed. I read that Urban Shocker pitched a perfect game for the Yanks, but someone who was at the game said it was a no-hitter. There's a difference, correct?"

Wilson nodded.

The man continued:

"A perfect game is twenty-seven batters up and twenty-seven batters set down. A rare feat. I was ecstatic for Urban Shocker. Imagine how I felt when I learned the truth."

He paused for effect.

"Betrayed."

"A no-hitter ain't nothing," Wilson remarked.

"Oh, I agree," the man said expansively. "I'm speaking here about the vast difference between what is said and what is true."

A second man appeared in the distance, treading lightly as he approached. The second man was dressed in the same manner as the first, though without the hat. He nodded to the man in the bowler and then smiled at Wilson.

"This young man agrees with me," the first man said.

"About what?" the second asked.

"Urban Shocker."

"Will you let that go?"

The elevator opened, and the two stepped inside without saying good-bye.

Wilson knocked and then opened the door to Martin Exports, expecting to find the dainty Mr. Jeffries. But Jeffries was not at his desk. The door to the exporter's office was closed, and Wilson knocked on the smoked glass. He could just make out the enormous form of the exporter in his chair, and before the exporter could claim that he was too busy to talk, Wilson pushed the door open. The exporter made no such excuse, though. Wilson saw that he'd been shot once through the forehead and once through the heart. A large reddish-brown stain in the shape of a sunflower spread across the exporter's shirt.

Wilson retreated and then sprinted down the hall. The elevator was stuck on the first floor, and so he plummeted down the stairs, passing two secretaries who were complaining about the crummy elevators in such a new building. When he reached the marble arcade foyer, he looked left toward Fifth Avenue and then right toward Broadway. Neither of the two men were in sight. He instinctively drifted toward the Fifth Avenue exit and pushed through the crowd, his eyes roving for any glimpse of the bowler hat.

"Excuse me!" a woman shouted as he stepped on her heel. The woman went down to one knee, and a crowd started to gather to assist her.

"Beg pardon," Wilson said under his breath.

He darted around the building and came out on the sunlit Broadway side. The light at Twenty-Third Street turned green right as a car's engine revved. The noise caught everyone's attention, and Wilson looked on with the rest of the spectators as the man in the bowler hat took the corner so quickly that the vehicle fishtailed and almost collided with an oncoming bus. Wilson raced to the intersection, but by the time he turned the corner, the car had disappeared into traffic.

26

MAX CHECKED THAT the temporary receptionist had taken her lunch hour. He unplugged the phone at its base so that no one would interrupt. The door to Miss Doling's darkened office was pulled shut, as it always was on a reading day. Sometimes she called from home to check for messages, but never during lunch, which she often took with friends at the Waldorf.

"It'll just be another moment," Mr. Ober was saying to the group assembled in his office. "We're waiting on one last person." He leaned against his desk and crossed his long legs, his palms resting behind him on the desktop.

The office was as crowded as a subway platform. Max had scavenged every extra chair from all corners of the Ober offices and even had to borrow one from the accountant whose practice was at the other end of the hall. He'd formed a semicircle around the boss's desk for those Ober had invited for the noon hour: Mrs. Anderson, Mr. Kelly, J. J. Clarke, Jeffries, and Anna Krupin, the chambermaid from the Byrne Hotel. Carmine Russo had come under the false pretense of pitching Ober ideas for books, which Ober had apologized for immediately. "I thought you might not come otherwise," he'd said. Russo had wanted to protest, but not in front of the others, who might spread the word that he was weak, an inclination Ober had counted on.

The party sat waiting silently, each annoyed but not wanting to draw attention by protesting.

The outer door creaked and Ober said:

"That'll be our man."

Max was surprised to see the cheery face of Arnold Sutton enter. Behind him a large, bearlike man with wary eyes and a unkempt beard followed.

"Here's your murderer!" Sutton announced dramatically. "Found him at that hotel by the seaport, like you said."

Mrs. Anderson gasped.

The large man's wide eyes scanned the room, lighting on Anna Krupin, whom he seemed relieved to see.

"No, no, Mr. Sutton," Ober said. "This is not—"

"But you said—"

The chambermaid spoke something in Russian, and the large man answered by nodding.

"This is Mr. Rosovsky," Ober said amiably. "He's Vera Rosovsky's husband."

Mr. Rosovsky noticed Mrs. Anderson and scowled in her direction.

"Max, will you please see that Mr. Rosovsky is made comfortable."

Max rolled his chair away from his desk and Mr. Rosovsky took it reluctantly. Max stood at the back of the room, by the door.

"You weren't exactly telling the truth when you said Mr. Rosovsky didn't come to New York," Ober said to Anna Krupin.

The chambermaid fidgeted in her seat.

Ober continued:

"Which is why you cleaned up all the evidence of whatever transgression occurred in the hotel room so immaculately, as if Vera had never checked in."

Anna nodded with a look of shame.

"We must ask ourselves: Was Mrs. Anderson also helping to conceal the fact that Mr. Rosovsky was in town?" Ober asked.

"I should say not!" Mrs. Anderson objected.

"No, I suppose not. After all, you were desperate to reunite Vera with Mr. Kelly, to make your foursome whole again, to recapture the glory of your first days in New York. Life hasn't been the same since the former Mrs. Kelly disappeared."

"And caused Mr. Kelly no end of trouble," Mrs. Anderson interjected.

Mr. Kelly gave a sheepish look.

"That's very charitable of you," Ober said, "but if I may, there's a more personal, more selfish reason guiding your interest in Vera's return."

"I don't know what you're speaking about."

"I'm speaking about your own husband's grudge against you, owing to Vera's behavior toward his half brother. Mr. Anderson has become cold and distant, and his frustrations are poisoning your marriage."

Mrs. Anderson gave an indignant look. "You've got a nerve."

"And you've got an excellent motive," Ober said.

The others in the room considered her, all eyes boring in. Anna Krupin translated the moment into Russian for Mr. Rosovsky, who moaned.

Mrs. Anderson gave a short reply in Russian, which startled both the chambermaid and the husband.

"Could she really have beaten Vera so savagely?" Sutton asked without regard to anyone's sensitivities.

Mrs. Anderson brought her hand to her mouth.

"I think you'll agree, Mr. Sutton, that in a fit of rage anyone is capable of anything. Especially if wielding a blunt instrument."

Sutton nodded sagely, as if he were Ober's equal in the matter.

"We know Mrs. Anderson knew that Vera was back in New York. We have her calling on Vera at the Byrne Hotel." Ober crossed his arms. "But who called on her, pretending to be her brother? This is a loose end that has defied resolution. But as we're all here . . .

Max, will you ask Sergeant Roosevelt to bring Miss Kennedy from the Byrne Hotel to our little gathering? She should be able to make an easy identification."

Max nodded and stepped out of the office.

"Can we trust the word of a hotel worker?" Clarke objected.

"I'll listen to any counterargument made by the accused," Ober said with a smile.

"Look here," Mr. Kelly said. "Is all of this show really necessary?"

Mr. Ober turned his attention in the direction of the complaint.

"Mr. Kelly, who prefers straight talk. A seemingly honest man who engaged in a dishonest scheme."

Mr. Kelly's face reddened.

"His sham marriage to Vera provided her the freedom from her old life in Russia. . . ."

Anna Krupin continued to translate the proceedings in Russian, and at the mention of Vera's marriage to Mr. Kelly, Mr. Rosovsky stood, stoically facing his adversary.

Ober swiftly moved through the chairs to Mr. Rosovsky and patted him on the shoulder. A pained look came across Mr. Rosovsky's face. He appeared tired and sank back into his chair.

"As I was saying"—Ober retook his position near his desk and continued his line of thought—"Mr. Kelly's pretend marriage to Vera and her subsequent disappearance have put him in a real bind with the federal government. He faces prison time if the ruse is discovered."

"You know about that, right, Carmine?" Sutton asked.

Russo turned in his chair and pierced Sutton's bravado with a glare.

"When I first met Mr. Kelly, I found his lack of sentiment for his late wife troubling," Ober continued. "After all, even if Mr. Kelly and Vera were not in love, they entered into a partnership and would at least, I'm sure, admit to being friends. And if a friend of mine had been murdered in such a way, well . . ."

No one in the room stirred.

"So Mr. Kelly's protestations are to be taken with a grain of the proverbial salt. I don't believe he wished, as Mrs. Anderson did, that Vera would return to their old arrangement, but it's easy to believe that Mr. Kelly, upon learning from Mrs. Anderson of Vera's return to New York, saw an opportunity to end his troubles with Immigration. Was it you who called on Vera at the Byrne Hotel, pretending to be her brother?"

"I think you know it wasn't me," Mr. Kelly said.

"As I said, I have no idea who that person was. With Miss Kennedy's help, we'll settle that matter to everyone's satisfaction. But by your own admission, you sent a note meant for Vera in care of Dilly's, so there's precedent for the idea that you were desperate to track her down. And you clearly knew that she'd left you for Carmine Russo. It's not hard to imagine a scenario where you finally catch up with her and beg for her help in resolving your legal problems. And it's easy to imagine her refusing, sending you into a murderous rage."

Mr. Kelly looked incredulous.

"And what about Carmine Russo? Vera swindled him out of a substantial amount of money pretending to be pregnant with his child."

Russo gave a wave, as if the money were trifling to him.

"Russo is a cruel man," Ober said, narrowing his eyes at the gangster. "A man of low integrity. I personally witnessed a piece of Russo's cruelty, a most demeaning humiliation of a mother and her son who were innocent of nothing more serious than playing the numbers. That they dared to try to collect their winnings from Mr. Russo was their great misfortune."

"Misfortune can be contagious," Russo warned.

Ober ignored the threat.

"And then there's the matter of Mr. Russo's associate, who was sent upstate when it was determined that the associate was paying too much attention to Vera."

"Who told you that?" Russo demanded.

"I was onto that piece of information too," Sutton piped up.

Russo regarded Sutton, who seemed to shrink inside his suit.

"So it was you she was hiding from," J. J. Clarke said.

"Ah, Mr. Clarke," Ober said. "Vera's onetime roommate whose passion for his tenant led him to write me an anonymous note pointing the investigation in his own direction, claiming to have vital information."

"She was a nice person who didn't deserve her fate," Clarke said softly. "I just wanted to make sure you knew that she was living in fear. But now it's all confused. The two husbands, and Mr. Russo . . ." He turned to Mr. Kelly. "I'm sorry if I had a wrong man, sir."

Mr. Kelly looked at Mr. Clarke as if he didn't exist, and certainly as if he and his opinions and apologies didn't matter.

The forceful presence of Sergeant Roosevelt appeared in the doorway.

"Miss Kennedy is here," he intoned.

"Please make her comfortable in the reception area," Ober said. "We'll call for her in a moment."

27

"Our victim's secret residency in Hell's Kitchen is a curious chapter in the matter. She leads Mr. Clarke to believe that she is living in fear for her life, but the man she's afraid of is a fictional character, an amalgamation of her first husband and, we can assume, Mr. Russo. One can imagine Vera scaring herself with such a creation and, more importantly, suffusing her stay with Mr. Clarke with an air of fear. Mr. Clarke has told us that she rarely left the apartment and took most of her meals at Chop Suey, the Chinese restaurant a floor below, though she did venture out at night for secretarial classes at Columbia University.

"At first blush, it seems curious that she would enroll herself as a night-school student, but if we can guess at her motives, it might have been to ensure that she was tucked out of sight during the evenings, when Mr. Russo and his associates conducted their business. It's a sure bet that an institution of higher learning was not on their usual nocturnal route."

Russo showed his teeth, but Ober just smiled condescendingly.

"The true purpose of these night classes will have to remain obscured," Ober went on. "But it's at Columbia that she met Mr. Jeffries, who offered Vera a job at Martin Exports. What made you offer her the position?"

Jeffries shrugged. "I thought she'd be good at the job."

"She evidently had a way with the opposite sex. Did you fall for her charms as well, Mr. Jeffries?"

"I'd like to think it was vice versa," Jeffries declared proudly.

"So you tried it on with her?"

"A gentleman never tells."

"I'm informed by a Miss Molly Adler that you're no gentleman," Ober shot back.

Jeffries grimaced.

"Miss Adler can point us to more than a few women who can testify firsthand about your so-called charms."

"This may come as a true shock to you, Mr. Ober," Jeffries said earnestly, "but whores lie."

Max watched his boss for a reaction, but there was none.

"There's very little you can tell me about the way of the world, Mr. Jeffries. And I've never believed a word, philosophical or otherwise, from anyone who substitutes violence for emotion."

"Are you sure that's what it's a substitute for?" Jeffries snickered.

"In all likelihood, it's a substitute for weakness."

Jeffries gripped the arms of his chair as if he might spring forward, but then thought better of it.

"You don't have anything you want to tell us, Mr. Jeffries?"

The room waited for an answer as Anna Krupin translated the question for Mr. Rosovsky under her breath.

"So what if I did?" Jeffries finally said. "She wasn't interested."

"And that was that?"

"She complained to my boss and he threatened to fire me."

"Did that make you mad?"

Jeffries considered the question.

"If I say that it did, you'll use that against me," he complained.

"If you say that it didn't, we're not likely to believe you anyhow," was the reply.

Ober and Jeffries remained in the standoff, and it was Ober who deflated the situation by turning away from Jeffries, telegraphing that Jeffries's admission, while left unexpressed, was duly recorded.

Ober addressed the room:

"In my business, I'm constantly evaluating character. Writers create characters, give them qualities that dictate their behaviors, and then put those characters in circumstances where the characters either act accordingly or actively fight against themselves. When a character acts contrary to his nature, the reader rightly cries foul, so it's my job to point out when a writer betrays a reader in this manner."

"But people act irrationally all the time," J. J. Clarke said.

"Yes, but irrational acts present themselves as just that. They are anomalies."

"I've heard of murders that sounded rash, or by chance."

"Again, it's possible. But the majority of murders fit a pattern. And the one certain thing we know about this murder is that it was quite clearly a crime of passion. Vera knew who killed her. She looked that person in the eyes. There may even have been a moment of terror when she anticipated it."

"This is all a bunch of talk," Russo said.

"Let's set aside the literary discussion. The point I'm trying to make is that this murder can easily be viewed as an inevitable albeit sad conclusion if we understand not only the character of the murderer, but also an aspect of the victim's character that may have contributed to her murder."

Mrs. Anderson stood. "I don't want to hear anything more about murder."

"If you please," Ober said, motioning for her to retake her seat. "We're all engaged in this unpleasant business, and we owe it to one another, and to Vera, to see it through."

Mrs. Anderson sat down again.

"Anna Krupin believed that Vera had fallen victim to her husband's rage, and was scared that she'd been complicit not in a romantic reunion, but in a violent confrontation. She tidied up the hotel room as if Vera had never checked in, stowing her luggage under a fictitious name, and then waited to see what would happen next. She even removed the room key from reception to give the impression that Vera had gone out of her own accord."

The chambermaid, who had been translating the entire proceedings, fell silent.

Ober smiled at her in a fatherly way.

"And while her motives may have been mixed, we can be glad she kept the luggage. For inside a zippered pocket we found three hundred dollars in cash. Not a very safe place to store this kind of money, but that is beside the point."

"That's *my* money," Russo said casually.

"That is the first true thing you've said. It *is* your money."

Ober walked around his desk and slid open one of the drawers, producing a white linen envelope. He flashed the front of the envelope. The name "Russo" was written in blue ink, underlined twice. He held the envelope out, and Russo hesitated before accepting it.

"I won't count it," Russo laughed, though no one else did.

Max imagined he saw a look of shame cross Russo's face as he pocketed the envelope.

"Why did she go to all the trouble?" J. J. Clarke asked. "Why didn't she just return the money at the outset?"

"Very astute question, Mr. Clarke."

Clarke looked pleased, as if he'd curried the favor of his favorite professor.

"This money is not the money she took from Carmine Russo. That money went to someone else."

Ober pivoted and addressed Anna Krupin.

"Will you please ask Mr. Rosovsky if he recently received money in the amount of three hundred dollars by wire transfer from his wife?"

Miss Krupin translated the question, and Mr. Rosovsky gave a fearful look.

"You can assure him that the money is his to keep," Ober added, guessing at the root of Mr. Rosovsky's concern.

She did so and Mr. Rosovsky nodded.

Ober continued:

"One of the aspects of this case that didn't add up was the trail of money. When I learned that Vera had taken three hundred dollars from Mr. Russo, it seemed like plenty of money to travel to Los Angeles and start a new life. But then why would she need to take a job at Martin Exports? And her employer told me that she lived in, well, let's say undesirable circumstances while in California. But in theory she should've had enough money to live. So if Vera was nearly broke out in Los Angeles, what happened to the money she took from Mr. Russo? A real puzzle, that, until I learned that Vera had . . . shall we say 'borrowed' . . . her husband's life savings in order to move to America."

Ober gave Mr. Kelly a smile, and Mr. Kelly nodded his thanks for this generalization.

"As the amounts were similar, I deduced that she'd used the money she swindled from Russo to repay her husband. And when I discovered yet another three hundred dollars in the zippered compartment in her luggage in an envelope addressed to Russo, the repayment scheme was apparent. My guess is she ended up feeling guilty about taking Russo's money and decided to find work to repay him, but then she needed money to move to Los Angeles, which was as far from New York as she could go without crossing yet another ocean. So she had to use the money she earned at Martin Exports for her move. Which helps us understand Vera's character a little better, that she had a sense of loyalty about her, and that she didn't forget an obligation, whatever the circumstances."

"But why did she need to go to Los Angeles?" Mr. Kelly asked.

"Perhaps Mr. Jeffries would like to speak to that."

"Perhaps I wouldn't," Jeffries answered.

"I'll testify on your behalf, then." To those assembled Ober said, "The true business of Martin Exports is espionage, and because she spoke Russian, Vera was hired to courier messages back and forth with a Russian double agent. And not long into her employ, but just before she disappeared, the double agent was murdered. Very dangerous work indeed. And now Mr. Jeffries's employer has been murdered as a result."

"I may be next!"

"Perhaps Sergeant Roosevelt will have some ideas on how best to navigate your predicament. I'm sure he will."

Ober found Roosevelt at the back of the room.

"Will you let Miss Kennedy know it'll be only another minute or two, please?"

Roosevelt nodded, and the floorboards creaked under his weight as he stepped out.

"The murder of the double agent is a plausible explanation for Vera's move to Los Angeles, but we can assume that the double agent never knew Vera's true identity. In fact, no one at Martin Exports knew her true identity."

Roosevelt returned to his post by the door.

Ober continued:

"My colleague, a film agent in Los Angeles who hired her as his personal secretary, knew her as Miss Vera Salzman. He had no way of knowing her given name was Vera Rosovsky. Or that Vera Rosovsky became Vera Kelly when she moved to America. Carmine Russo knew her as Vera Miller. She rented an apartment in Hell's Kitchen from Mr. Clarke as Miss Vera Smith." He turned to Jeffries. "What did she call herself at Martin Exports?"

"Vera Clarke."

J. J. Clarke gave a start.

"How flattering," he said.

"I thought you might be pleased to hear that, Mr. Clarke. After all, you were in love with Vera, weren't you?"

Clarke blushed, betraying his words:

"I most certainly was not."

"When I was in your apartment, you'll remember you showed us your studio, a space nearly filled with canvases. What was remarkable to me about your paintings was that they were all of the same woman. And I think a closer inspection of your work will reveal that the figure that features so prominently in your work is that of the woman you knew as Vera Smith."

Clarke snorted. "What can you possibly know about art? I'd advise you to stick to the realm of the written word. You're expert at spinning fantasy, it seems."

Ober asked Jeffries: "Why did Vera tell you she wanted the job?"

"She said she needed to make a lot of money quickly."

"Did she say why she needed to make it quickly?"

"No."

"After all, while she repaid Mr. Rosovsky, she felt no compunction to do it quickly."

Clarke pointed at Russo.

"She probably needed it to get away from him!" he said. "A husband thousands of miles away is one thing, but a vicious man like Russo won't wait months to be repaid."

Ober said: "But as far as Mr. Russo knew, she had already left for California. So in theory, she wasn't in any danger from Mr. Russo."

"She said she was afraid of her husband," Clarke said feebly.

"But she told you that her husband berated her in Russian. And since Mr. Kelly does not speak Russian, we can see that she was acting out a role, that of a scared wife in fear of her husband. One can ask himself, why would she need to take on this persona?"

Ober paused and scrutinized the faces assembled for the hint of revelation and then said:

"Perhaps to protect herself from the unwanted advances of her landlord."

"You're mad," Clarke said. "Completely certifiable."

"Yet again we can turn to characterization. I asked myself what kind of person would send an anonymous note telling on himself, with the sole intention of involving himself in the case."

"I told you, I wanted you to know about the husband."

"You could've simply sent an anonymous note about that fact. No, you bid me to come to your apartment, to inject yourself into the middle of the case. You're a man who must control his circumstances. And when Vera rebuffed your advances, you lost that control. It must've driven you wild. You told me that Miss Smith spent most of her time in her room. I submit that was to avoid you, who had become more than a nuisance. More like a cancer."

"Wrong."

"I also submit that she was desperate to get away. Her plan to ride out her fake pregnancy fell apart almost immediately, owing to the advances of Mr. Clarke, and she needed to make money fast. And then along comes the job offer from Martin Exports. Excellent pay for dangerous work. She quickly amassed the money she needed and abruptly left for California."

"So the timing was a coincidence?" Jeffries asked.

Ober nodded.

"This is an amusing fiction you're creating," Clarke scoffed. "Is this how you work with your writers? Spinning fabrications from supposition? I'm not one of your writers."

"You must've been furious when she abandoned you without notice. You knew immediately that it wasn't that she couldn't afford the rent. By your own admission, you pay well below market rate for your apartment. But in your own deluded mind you believed she was more than a roommate."

Clarke stood up so quickly he knocked his chair over. The crash reverberated throughout the rapt room.

"Take your seat, Mr. Clarke," Sergeant Roosevelt commanded.

Clarke sat back down.

Ober said: "We can feel some sympathy for Vera. She is desperate to get out of Russia, so she steals her husband's money and comes to America. But then her conscience gets the better of her, and she cons Mr. Russo out of the necessary amount to repay the stolen money. She takes the apartment in Hell's Kitchen—maybe to lie low and deceive Mr. Russo into believing she's in California, or maybe to allow her time to find work and make the money she needs to repay Mr. Russo as she had her husband—but in short order she's again desperate to flee her situation. She gets the money together and moves as far away as she can, where she's employed by my colleague, Mr. Swenson. She starts her life anew and also sets aside a little money every week to repay her debt to Mr. Russo. Then Mr. Swenson invites her to accompany him to New York, and because of what we know about Vera Rosovsky's nature, we can assume that the idea of returning to New York brings with it the feeling of guilt about the way she left things with Mr. Clarke. And when she's set to return to the city, she lets him know that she'll be in town. She wants to have lunch and clear the air. The waiter at Chop Suey told us that he'd seen Vera recently, which didn't mean anything at the time. He could've simply been mistaken. He couldn't be sure of an exact date. But the two of you had lunch, and Vera asked you to forgive her. Even though anyone could see that she had nothing to be forgiven for. She thought an apology and a nice lunch would be the end of it, but she had no way of knowing that in her absence your obsession had only grown."

"Nope."

"You brought her up to the apartment under the pretense of showing her the work you'd been doing. Believing lunch had cleared the air, she agreed. But when she saw the canvases with her likeness, she realized, too late, that she'd walked into a trap. What happened next, Mr. Clarke?"

"You tell me."

"She pretended that she had to leave."

"It's almost as if you were there," Clarke said sarcastically.

"But you weren't going to let her leave, were you? She'd run out on you once before, and you weren't going to let that happen again."

Clarke sat silently.

"What happened when she tried to leave?" Ober asked again.

"If she would've just let me show her how much I loved her."

"If you'd loved her, you wouldn't have terrorized her."

"It was her who terrorized me!"

"But it was you who knocked her to the floor, and it was you who, in a blind rage, wailed away at her until you'd beaten the life out of her."

Clarke lunged violently at Ober, and Max flinched. He saw the distressed look on his boss's face, but Clarke tripped over the outstretched legs of Jeffries, who was merely trying to get out of the way of the melee. Sergeant Roosevelt expertly navigated the chairs and corralled the forlorn artist.

"I loved her," he said as Roosevelt pushed him toward the door.

"I doubt it was love," Ober said, regaining his composure.

Roosevelt led Mr. Clarke away, and order descended on the room again.

"Poor Vera," Mrs. Anderson said quietly.

Anna Krupin translated Mrs. Anderson's words for Mr. Rosovsky and he shook his head. Mrs. Anderson left her chair and huddled with the chambermaid and Vera's husband. Mr. Rosovsky spoke to Mrs. Anderson in Russian and she nodded.

"Are you finished with us?" she asked.

Ober nodded, and without further fanfare, they departed.

"Same for me?" Russo asked.

"You've got your money," Ober said coldly.

"Another successful business transaction," Russo said smartly. Then: "She needn't have gone to all the trouble. I wouldn't have pressed her for the money."

"Perhaps she saw you as the rest of us do," Ober remarked.

"As I said, it's just business. I'm an upstanding member of the business community."

"Which is why dead bodies end up on your doorstep," Sutton added.

Russo disregarded Sutton's comment. The outer door slammed behind him.

28

"WHAT PUT YOU ONTO THE ARTIST?" Sutton asked.

"None of the narratives, while suggestive, seemed to satisfy the details of this case completely. As compelling as the individual strands were, they weren't a coherent story. And then I paid a visit to Molly Adler's—"

"Don't let the scandal sheets get a hold of that information!" Sutton kidded.

Jeffries was annoyed by Sutton's clowning.

"Strictly professional," Ober said. "I had a nice conversation with that lady, and I noticed one of Clarke's paintings on the walls, which meant he was a patron. His presence in this matter at first seemed faint, but when I saw the painting, it occurred to me that Clarke was at the heart of the case. How else did you, Mr. Sutton, also a patron, learn that Vera was taking secretarial classes at Columbia? The police didn't know this information. Only Clarke knew."

"Mr. Jeffries knew too," Max reminded him.

"Yes, but Mr. Jeffries was serving a lengthy ban from Miss Adler's establishment during these events. I noted that neither Mr. Jeffries nor Mr. Sutton gave a look of acknowledgment, subtle or otherwise, when they assembled here today."

"It wasn't a ban," Jeffries protested.

"You should know, Mr. Jeffries, that Sergeant Roosevelt is aware of your ... proclivities, and he's not on anyone's payroll. He's his own man and doesn't take kindly to men like you."

"I'm also my own man," Jeffries said. "I don't have to listen to any more lectures from you."

He left without anyone objecting.

Mr. Kelly, who had remained seated while others had stood to leave, finally rose to his feet.

"Thank you for your efforts, Mr. Ober," he said. "I appreciate your finding some measure of justice for Vera. I didn't know her as well as some might suppose, but what I did know about her, I liked. I'll always wonder if there was something I could've done to prevent her fate."

"I wish you well, Mr. Kelly. Yours isn't an easy road," Ober said.

"By my own hand," Mr. Kelly said without pity.

"I've spoken to a friend at Immigration, who would like you to call on him. He might be able to help you clear up the matter to the satisfaction of the government. Max has the information."

Max handed a folded piece of paper to Mr. Kelly, who accepted it gratefully. He shook hands with Mr. Ober and left.

"The poor woman," Sutton said with a surprising touch of earnestness.

"It's very unfortunate," Ober allowed. He was not given to sentiment, Max knew, and especially not with someone like Sutton, for whom Ober had a casual disdain.

"My cousin told me the body has gone missing," Sutton said.

Ober started, remembering something. "Perhaps you can be of help in that matter."

Sutton tried unsuccessfully to mask his eagerness. "Anything."

"Sergeant Roosevelt relayed to me that a Jane Doe was found in one of the reservoirs. Would it be possible for you to arrange for Mr. Rosovsky to view the body before he returns to Russia?"

"But I don't speak Russian."

"But you know someone who does," Ober reminded him. "I'm

sure Miss Krupin will assist you."

Sutton nodded solemnly. "You can count on me."

Ober walked Sutton to the door. The temporary receptionist nodded a hello when she opened the door, back from her lunch.

Sutton screwed up his face. "The hotel clerk must've gotten bored and left."

Ober grinned.

Sutton's face fell.

"Miss Kennedy couldn't remember who called on Vera that day. There's some confusion about whether or not anyone ever did call on her, pretending to be her brother."

"A bluff!" Sutton's voice was full of admiration.

23

Max spread the newspaper out on his desk, blowing on the cup of hot chocolate he'd bought to warm his hands on the walk to work from the subway. A sip of the boiling liquid had scalded his tongue, and he worried the spot back and forth against the roof of his mouth in an effort to start the healing.

A gust of wind blew in through the window near Mr. Ober's desk. The crisp smell of fall was definitely in the air. The window would remain open all winter long, though, as a release valve for the building's heaters, which ran day and night and turned unventilated offices into ovens.

Max perused the newspaper, his eyes landing on the headline: MURDER-SUICIDE IN YONKERS. His insides were pulled tight as he read about how Jeannette Barnes had taken the train to Yonkers, knocked on the door of the Slater residence, and fired at Philip Slater point-blank when he answered the door. Max jolted up out of his seat when he read the next line, that Jeannette had then turned the gun on herself. The two bodies had been lying on top of each other when the police arrived, finding a desolate Mrs. Slater with her infant son.

"It's not your fault."

Miss Doling emerged from the doorway.

Max looked up from the paper and squinted, as if he didn't

recognize her. His eyes brimmed with tears. Miss Doling wrapped her arms around him and he wilted, his suddenly wet cheeks pressed against her neck. The door to reception opened with the creak Max had been meaning to speak to the building super about, and he and Miss Doling parted, Max wiping his cheeks on his sleeves. Miss Doling gave him a smile and nodded. Max folded the newspaper into his top desk drawer as Mr. Ober entered.

"Good morning, boss," Miss Doling greeted him.

"Good morning all."

Miss Doling slipped out as quietly as she'd arrived, and Max sat behind the screen, staring at his desktop, the shock still fresh.

"Let's send a telegram to Mr. Swenson."

"Of course, sir."

"And I'd like you to return these catalogs to the printer," Ober said. "Please explain to him that our borrowing them was necessary for a vital matter."

"Yes, sir."

"Also, I'm expecting a contract for Scott's new story, and he needs us to turn it around quickly. Will you see if you can induce the contract so I'll have it for the weekend? Otherwise I'll be forced to advance him the money until payment is rendered."

Ober smiled. He'd had to loan Fitzgerald money on a number of occasions, though Fitzgerald had always repaid the amounts.

The phone on Max's desk rang. The new temporary receptionist spoke into his ear, and he must've had a strange look on his face, because his boss asked: "What is it?"

"Mr. Schellinger is here to see you."

Ober put down the file folder he'd been perusing.

"Show him in, please."

DON'T MISS!

Murder at the Carousel Club:
A Harold Ober Mystery

by J. D. West

The annual Winter Ball at the Carousel Club in Central Park gathers New York's most prominent citizens together for an evening of dance, dinner, and frivolity. Invitations are coveted among the elite, and whispers about who is attending and, of equal interest, who is not are an annual parlor game played out in the salons of the rich and powerful.

When Harold Ober reluctantly accepts his invitation, he regrets the decision almost immediately upon setting foot in the gaudy nightclub. And once he learns that millionaire playboy Arthur Schellinger, recently acquitted in the murder of his girlfriend, is seated at his table, his regret is magnified.

As the evening wears on, Ober begins to plan his escape. But unbeknownst to the revelers, an epic snowstorm is barreling down on the city, one that will paralyze its residents for days. Soon the guests realize they are trapped inside the evening's carnival. And when Arthur Schellinger is found murdered, everyone is a suspect. Including Harold Ober himself!

Made in USA - North Chelmsford, MA
1343468_9781521171073
022 0938